THE OLD MAN AND THE VOID

Karina Fabian

LASER COW PRESS

Laser Cow Press

Merritt Island, FL

Laser Cow Press
Merritt Island, FL
https://fabianspace.com

Book Layout © 2017 BookDesignTemplates.com
Cover Design by Dawn Grimes

The Old Man and the Void/Karina Fabian. – 1st ed.
Print ISBN 978-1-7334471-2-6

For those who face incredible odds each day and keep going, and for those who refuse to be defined by their mistakes.

"But man is not made for defeat. A man can be destroyed but not defeated."

—THE OLD MAN AND THE SEA
ERNEST HEMINGWAY, 1952

Contents

Chapter One

Dex dreamed of the warblers—and of Scarlet.

He climbed up the craggy trail of Squatty Mountain, thrilling at the strength of his young body. The path was too familiar to be a challenge any longer, but today wasn't about pushing his limits anyway. He had a different test in mind.

He paused at a flat spot and looked back toward the brown-haired beauty struggling up the rise.

"Whoever named this 'Squatty Mountain' should be shot!" she declared. She had her hands against the steep incline, and she tilted her head just enough that he could see her glare.

"He was," Dex told her. "Barfight, though that's not what our history books say. Not much farther."

"This is not my idea of a date," she grumbled at him. "Just because I'd never been planetside didn't mean I needed to see this much planet." She took a few more steps, as if to prove that his home's real gravity and real atmosphere would not conquer her, then paused, one foot upslope, elbow braced against the bent knee as she caught her breath.

Grinning, he held out his hand.

She gave him a dirty look, and for a moment, he thought she'd slap it away. Then, with a grimace that said, "I'm humoring you; that's all," she took his hand and allowed him to pull her up.

He took the opportunity to pull her close as well.

"It's worth it. You'll see. But you have to keep quiet from here on," he whispered in her ear, then released her. He knew she thought he'd kiss her then. He wanted to kiss her, but first, the warblers. If she understood about them and him, their next kiss would be the kiss that changed everything. "Stay low."

Nonetheless, as they came to the crest of the mountain, she stood gaping at the view until he had to yank her down before she was seen. "I said to stay low!" he hissed.

Instead of snapping a protest, she gave him a glare that was half apology and followed him at a crawl to where they could peek over the cliff. She could take directions, follow his lead. Just one more indication that she was the one.

He peered over the rock ledge and grinned. He'd checked with the global parks satellite to make sure the pterodactyl-like creatures had returned to the nesting grounds, but a part of him imagined taking Scarlet all this way for nothing but empty rock cliffs and a towering waterfall—romantic enough in itself, but not suiting his purpose. But the flock was there, occupying caves, soaring in lazy circles, some diving in and out of the cascading water. He didn't see any hatchlings, but they tended to keep to the shadows of the caves or their mothers' wings.

One adult male emerged from the lake, its beak sac full of water and fish. Huge leathery wings beat the air with gentle puffs that belied their enormous power. He rose above the others, then belched its prize. Silver fish shimmered as they fell. The flock swirled and dove after them, taking small pecks out of their scaly flesh, making a game out of their snack. The first warbler hovered above them all and called out encouragement with the gurgling roar that gave the warblers their name.

Heart racing, he turned to see Scarlet watching with disbelief and wide-eyed wonder.

"Dex!" she exclaimed.

"Dex!" Santiago's voice jerked him to wakefulness, the dream lost in the past. "Dex. You must wake up now."

"I wasn't asleep," he grumbled. "I was thinking."

"Of course. We're about to enter the swarls."

"Got it." Dex stood, bones creaking in protest, and shook off the last of his "thinking" as he activated the sensors that would tie him to the ships' systems. He positioned himself in the middle of the bridge, arms outstretched, legs braced, ready.

"Show me."

The map materialized around him, filling the space of the bridge. Instead of a small indicator to show the ship's position, he stood in the place of the *Santiago*. Their senses combined, he heard the messages picked up by the ship's comms: scavengers calling to each other, simple hails to claim a day's territory or merely to assure each other that there was life in the ancient graveyard. Piggybacking some of the signals were the transmissions of the aliens who had fought and died, taking two civilizations with them. A lot of ships tuned them out, letting the computer analyze the direction and degradation to determine if the transmission might have come from a worthy catch.

Dex, however, let them play. Over the years, he'd come to know their cadence, to recognize the difference between Civilization A and Civilization B, as the historians had so uniquely labeled them. He could even imitate the sounds, although he had no idea what he was saying. No one did; there was no Rosetta stone to provide a clue to the language of races dead millennia before humans had entered this quadrant. The closest anyone or anything ever came to communication with the artifacts was his own ship, and Santiago insisted it was not so much communication as learning which buttons to push.

Scarlet had always found that especially funny.

For the moment, however, human traffic was heavy, and the ghosts were still.

"You woke me early," he complained to his ship.

"You weren't sleeping. However, you should eat before we begin, and you must take your medications."

"I'm fine," he protested, but he slipped his sandals on and padded into the kitchen. He ate a simple meal on automatic, swallowed down the requisite pharmaceuticals, settled in the medical chair, and allowed himself to be checked out while he sipped a third cup of coffee. The results looked the same as last month—not good—and the medical bot reminded him that he still had another rejuv treatment waiting on Keldar Station.

Those had been another gift from Molly, a futile attempt to keep him around forever. He'd chided her on the waste of money.

"We're still a century away from real rejuvenation—if such youth is even possible. You can't beat time," he'd told her, but in the end, she'd worn him down and he'd accepted the gift. She may have been apprenticed to him to learn how to navigate the accretion disk, but from Scarlet, she'd learned to navigate his moods with equal skill. Besides, he hated to see her worry.

Which is why he had not told her he had Disk Activated Memory Disorder. Modern medicine may have found a way to stave off the ravages that changing gravitational fields inflicted on the body, but it had not found a cure for what those shifting fields did to the mind. Seasoned hunters called it "the mind swarls" for how they ensnared you in your own memories. The acronym, DAMD, was accurate, too.

He had to admit, he had felt spryer after the last one. His eyes had rejected the treatment, but his skin itched less—he scratched at his scarred arm—but youth? He'd left that behind. That was fine, too; his time of scaling mountains and making love were past.

He stood, stretched his old bones, and went to relieve himself.

He'd just returned to the bridge and had again doffed his shoes when they received the hail.

"*Grissom's Charge* to *Santiago*. Getting a little close there, aren't you, Old Man?"

"Nope," he replied, voice flat and distracted. His hands moved in a familiar pattern as he outlined a sector of the Disk then stretched the pattern to extend the lines in a funnel toward the event horizon. With another hand movement, he transmitted the map of space he'd marked. "Claiming this as mine for the year, subjective to you— more if need be. Don't need assistance, just the freedom to do my job."

The captain of *Grissom's Charge* grunted. The motto of the independent trader didn't mean as much to Union Men, but that didn't mean they didn't respect it. "Copy that. Be advised: Union ships have been told to exercise restraint when it comes to you. Don't expect anyone to go haring off to rescue you if you do something crazy."

"I understand and thank you for that."

"Do not be concerned for us," Santiago added. "We know the tricks, and Dex's resolution is second to none."

The Charge's captain barked a laugh. "Copy that, Santiago. Good hunting."

Hunting. There was a man who understood. "Roger, *Grissom's Charge*. Same to you."

When the other ship logged off, he turned back to business: a small course correction, then a quick diagnostic. He sighed at the results. "I'm sorry, my friend. You are old and in need of repair, yet I must put you under stress once again."

"I am programmed to serve. Besides, I have my tricks. I am not so different from you."

The Old Man chuckled. "Then let's go in."

The floorboards rumbled slightly under his feet as the engines engaged. It sent a thrill along his spine, making him feel young again—or at least younger. He pushed the feelings aside. Right now, he had to concentrate on his prey and on the swirling currents of matter before him. Once upon a time, scientists had thought the accretion disk of a black hole was a fairly homogeneous donut-shaped swirl of "star stuff" and gas, getting shredded past the atomic level, pulling time and space with it in its dance to destruction.

Over the centuries, they realized there was a complexity to an accretion disk—thicker surges of matter, X-rays and gamma rays flying out at incredible speed and power from areas closer to the event horizon, even small pockets of cool gases surrounded by hotter gasses that shot out of the disk like bullets from a gun. "Cold bullets" someone had dubbed them even before the age of interstellar travel, and the name had stuck.

Yet still, one constant remained: matter flowed toward and into the singularity, moving in a tightening spiral until it fell into the information vacuum that was the black hole itself. Something powerful enough might escape, flying or fighting its way up along the current of matter, but nothing ever went against the current. Never. The bending of time and space along the black hole, called "frame drag" by the ancient astronomers, did not allow matter, not even light, to go against the current.

Until Lincoln Eriadne and its Discordian Accretion Disk.

This black hole didn't follow the stately dance of demise like its fellows. Here, matter fought and tangled, snarled against invisible gravity barriers and defied the frame drag. Rather than a smoothly rushing whirlpool, Lincoln Eriadne was a wild river with rapids and eddies and smaller whirlpools of matter dubbed "swarls," sometimes flowing in groups, flinging matter between them in a kind of mad reel. And not just any matter, but the remains of ancient ships from a long-dead civilization.

The relic hunters had named the worst sector the "Zone."

The Zone took up a roughly diamond-shaped "slice" of the accretion disk. Most astrophysicists considered it akin to a storm in a gas giant: huge, violent, slow to dissipate but natural and doomed to surrender to the overpowering forces of the black hole. The Union declared it off-limits. Most hunters gave it a grudging respect, patrolling outside its forces in hopes it would spew out an artifact caught in its tumult.

The impossibility of it had attracted scientists for nearly a century and led to the founding of a university station that studied it at a safe distance. Keldar Research Station, where Dex and Scarlet had lived for nearly a decade, she monkeying with shield technology while he sought to discover how something had survived the spaghettification and was creating pockets of its own gravity.

Dex had been in love with the Disk almost as long as he'd been in love with Scarlet. He'd made the Zone his life's focus. It had led him to finding his first artifact, purchasing the *Santiago*, and leaving university life with its bureaucratic demands. Instead, he'd devoted himself to studying the Disk— when not chasing relics to make enough money to get by. Scarlet—adaptable, adventurous Scarlet—left her work to join in his.

Since Scarlet had died, "getting by" had become easier. She'd always insisted on two weeks in port every six months to refurbish the *Santiago*, to shop, and to meet other scientists face-to-face. "You need human contact, Dex. I need human contact." Of course, she'd always insisted on the fanciest suite the station had available where they shared plenty of human contact.

With her gone, he didn't bother. Food had lost its appeal, becoming mere nourishment. He liked the quiet of the ship, and as his vision degraded, he preferred the comfort of familiar surroundings. He still had the challenge of the Zone to keep him on his toes, and the knowledge that his finds advanced the progress of humankind motivated him. He consulted with physicists over the comms. Without Scarlet, there was no point to a fancy suite.

Nonetheless, a latent guilt rose in him as he looked around Santiago's dingy, worn interior.

"*After* this catch, let's make for University Port, maybe even Keldar Station, get you a good refurb," he told the ship.

"An excellent idea." Did he hear glee or relief in the AI's tone?

"After this catch. We'll need the money." He returned his attention to the images around him, seeking any tell-tale sign of the alien ship.

He'd only caught glimpses of the ship in the past, but he knew it outsized and outclassed anything they'd seen before. It had to have been trapped deep within the accretion disk, its miracle of shielding keeping it from being torn to quantum-sized shreds when even its own planet had spaghettified.

An image flashed in his mind: Scarlet, head tilted back, laughing in delight at the word. "Spaghettified?"

"Yes." He'd sighed, exasperated. How impatient he had been then! "When you get too close to the black hole, you get stretched by the gravity. Get too close, and the difference between the gravity of say, your right side and your left, will be enough to pull you long and thin—"

"—like spaghetti?" she concluded and laughed again.

Had he noticed then how she sparkled when she laughed? Even now, he remembered his irritation. Spaghettification had just destroyed the probe the university had sent in, before the probe had gathered the data he'd so badly needed for his thesis. He was going to have to rewrite the entire thing into something dull and inconclusive if he wanted to graduate. But she'd continued to laugh and suck in her dinner noodles with exaggerated puckers until he'd thrown down his fork in disgust and left the room, wondering why he'd married such a silly woman.

He didn't want to remember that part, or the day of stony silence that followed. Instead, he focused on her laugh, the whiteness of her teeth, her face flushed with mirth, and then remembered the pensive concentration on her face when, days later, he'd caught her reading one of his textbooks...

"Dex! Cold bullet to starboard!"

Chapter Two

Santiago's warning jerked Dex's attention back to reality even as the ship jerked to avoid the hazard.

"Got it," Dex snarled, though the hammering of his heart claimed otherwise. Nonetheless, his body had sensed it and jerked itself and the ship aside. He let Santiago finish the maneuver, then took back the helm. The bullet might only have been a small pocket of gas, but the power with which it surged through the Disk could tear a normal ship apart.

Not the *Santiago*, of course. It did have tricks; in this case, powerful shielding, designed by Scarlet and built by her family, that protected it from the extreme velocity impacts of the spaghettified remains of two planetary systems, as well as the spaghettification process itself. Even more, she and Dex had adapted the shield generator of a relic he had captured early in his career, mastering it through trial and error as much as genius. While the university and the Union still puzzled over the others they'd acquired, she and Dex had outfitted their new ship, the *Santiago*, with a working CivB shield. The *Santiago* might be old, but he could dive more deeply into the Disk and ride its turbulent spacetime waves like no other ship in commission. A cold bullet would have tumbled them and knocked them off course; dangerous in this part of the stream, but not destructive.

"Did you send out an area warning?" Dex asked his ship's AI.

"Already done. *Eternal* acknowledges, with thanks."

Dex grunted. "Swarl approaching. We'll hold and see what it turns up."

"Would you like to sit?" Santiago asked. "It's been two hours."

Had it? Even for two objects in the same time stream, time was relative. "I'm good for a while longer."

"I understand, but we should both conserve energy for the catch."

He started to argue, but his legs concurred with Santiago's suggestion. He gave in to their logic. "Hold relative position," he ordered as he left the nav field to fetch a chair—the comfortable wheeled one he could push away if things got intense. At Santiago's next suggestion—seconded by his stomach—he went into the kitchen and fetched a bottle of water and a couple of meal bars and slid them into the side pocket of the chair. He settled in and held out his arms, palms up. The holographic navigation field lowered so that he sat in the same space as the *Santiago*.

His hands moved over the field, investigating the swirls and eddies as they thundered past the ship, dragging it with them.

"Dex, four o'clock," Santiago called, using the ancient directional system that still proved useful where north and south did not exist. Dex twisted his head to the right to see a small group of shadows approaching, weaving their way through the matter stream like fish on a migration.

"What the..." His voice trailed off as Santiago identified and gave a temporary designator to each of the objects. Relics, each one, the small weapon drones of Civilization A. Never had he seen so many, so close or so intact. He directed Santiago to focus sensors temporarily in that direction.

"Are we changing target?" the AI asked.

He bit his lip as he looked over the readings, sucking on his teeth in thought. They might be able to catch two or three, especially if they snuck in behind and took the stragglers. He'd never seen any in such good shape; and if he hadn't, no one had. They'd make a great catch.

But not the catch—not the one he'd settled his sights on. Maybe, if Molly and her crew were here, together they could have snagged them and still had time for the ship. But alone...

"No," he decided. "Tag their vectors and spacetime stamps and pass the information to Molly and to the *Eternal*. Let them have the small fry. We've got bigger plans today."

"Acknowledged. Plenty to share."

He glanced again at the ships, and his fist clenched. They hardly seemed damaged by time in the Disk. What could humans learn if they had intact relics like these?

He saw Scarlet sitting at the console, slouching back, her head tilted over her shoulder so she could look at him. Her hair shone in the artificial light of the bridge, and her eyes sparkled with love and admiration.

"You and your mysteries. You haven't lost your need to find something new." Her memory chuckled.

"Still haven't," he muttered to himself, as his hands roved the swell. They'd found dozens of relics, to be sure, even adapted their shield technology to protect the *Santiago*, but they still hadn't unlocked their secrets. The small ships that escaped the Disk were too damaged, and they lacked any ordinary common-ground records that might help humans unlock the language of either alien race. In fact, they only guessed that there were two races or species at war based on the disparate sizes and shapes of the ships as well as the stylistic differences of the languages.

He grunted to himself. Leave the language to the linguists. Even the physics had progressed past his understanding. That wasn't who he was, anyway. Scarlet had seen that early on, on the cliffs of Squatty Mountain. "You'll never be satisfied just thinking about someone else's discoveries," she'd told him when he debated about applying to Keldar. "You want to be out there, hunting down the data yourself."

Pretty Scarlet with pretty wavy hair. Where had she gone? I need to talk to her about Keldar, ask her to go with me...

"Dex?"

He jerked at the sound of the ship's voice, out of the memory, back to reality. He blinked to find himself half-rising from his chair. The colorful miasma around him confused him.

"Dex, are you all right?"

"I..." *Dex. That's my name. And the ship?*

"Dex. You're onboard the Santiago. Do you remember me?"

"Of course, I remember you," he snarled. He sank back into the chair. His hands shook, and his breath came fast and shallow. He felt a tingle on his wrist and looked at the blue medical band. The digital display noted the time and date and amount of medication it had just dosed him with.

Damned mind swarls. He closed his eyes and waited for the present to return to him.

"Better?" Santiago asked.

"It's too quiet in here," he countered. "Too easy to daydream. Let's hear the Outside."

"As you wish."

The squelches and staccato hissing of static assaulted his ears, but he grinned and settled himself more attentively in the chair. Plenty of ways to pick up patterns. Visual was easiest, and the natural default of humans. As his sight had declined, he'd turned to other methods: the sensations of the nav field, certainly, but also sound.

"Come on," he breathed. "You can play hide-and-seek among the matter, but can you run silent?"

Lowering his gaze and letting his eyes unfocus, he concentrated on the noise of X-ray frequencies translated into hearing range and of the friction sounds of high-speed matter. He could hear the patterns, and long years of practice had helped him distinguish what each sound meant. One by one, he ordered Santiago to filter them out: First, the echoes of calls between hunter ships, some recent, some phantoms of messages misdirected and trapped in the Disk. Then, the chitters and moans of the alien ships. Once, linguists had hoped for some breakthrough but now ruled that these were simple "friend or foe" signals or SOS beacons. Nonetheless, they proved useful enough. One by one, Santiago dismissed those they recognized as belonging to a smaller, known drone type. The one they wanted sang its own song.

"There! Wait...now! Do you have it?"

"I do." The AI replayed the sound, and when Dex grunted agreement, added, "I am determining position. It's rounding the swarl."

On the nav field, a small, cigar-shaped icon started a slow curve up.

"Ha! We have you now! Engines full. Shields to maximum. We'll have to get it before it tops that swell. We can use the momentum to push us out."

"I know the drill."

Santiago's reply might have irritated Dex on another day, but this time, his focus had narrowed on their prize. He stood and kicked away the chair, the better to feel the motion of the ship and compare it to the changes of the nav field and the rhythms of the static over the loudspeaker. There were no interruptions this time, no Union ships in his way.

He licked lips gone dry with excitement.

"It's you and me, Scarlet," he muttered. "With Santiago, we'll bring back a ship the likes of which no one has seen. Careful!" His hand twisted sharply on the course, directing the Santiago away from a gamma wave that would have disrupted their shields. The ship rocked, the change too abrupt for the lowered inertial dampeners to compensate for. He staggered but caught his balance quickly.

"I saw it," the AI replied neutrally. "Please do not jerk my systems." Almost as a scold, he felt the ship sway more gently as it avoided a second wave.

"Keep sharp, then. Capture beam charged?"

"Yes," Santiago replied. "And the grapplers are primed. The ship is too large for the Mag Net."

"Get ready to relay that power to the beam if needed, then. We've done captures without a net before." Dex grinned. The only relics caught in his lifetime were the small, automated drones and some debris of larger ships. But their target was much larger. Crew sized. What would the exobiologists think when he brought back an actual alien?

In the nav field, the alien ship had grown to the size of his hand. He closed his eyes and reached out, judging through sound and touch the turbulence of the matter streaming between it and him. The ship was still far enough away that the dragging of space and time was pulling it ahead, despite the curling disturbance between them. "We need more speed. Take us down."

"Into the swarl?"

"Yes! We'll use the current to rush us toward the ship and snag it on the upsweep.

We'll use that momentum to push us both away and out of the Zone." Quickly, his fingers traced a general path, leaving the AI to handle the details. Even in the height of his mathematical prowess, he could not have traced the exact route in time. He didn't know if anyone could. It took an AI to handle all the variables.

But I'm the one who saw the path, he thought with grim satisfaction. "There. Perfect the route."

"I have it. Brace yourself. This could get bumpy."

He felt the deck drop slightly as the *Santiago* moved into the backflow of matter circling the gravity bump. Around him, the nav field expanded and he was swept up in a rushing torrent of red and orange waves. He pulled his arms in, feeling the resistance. He set one hand, palm flat, to his side, gauging the flow, while his other hand stretched straight out, pointing their path like a compass needle. The cacophony of sensory impressions dizzied him. He growled for Santiago to turn off the noise.

"Where's the ship?" he demanded. The expanded view had pushed it from sight.

Santiago supplied a vector and a small "window" with a compressed view of the matter swell that showed the ships' positions.

"It's doing what it's supposed to," Dex spoke aloud. "Good. Once we round the bottom of this swarl, pull in toward the gravity well. We'll pass it on the inside and fire the beam."

"We're coming under the convertor corona," Santiago warned.

Dex glanced up and to his right to where the bluish-white hologram marked the swirling superhot gasses that hovered over the inner part of the Disk. The radiation from the corona wreaked havoc with the communications. He didn't know if it'd affect the beam; no one ever hunted this close to the black hole.

Dex lowered his gaze to the aching blackness that marked the black hole lurking starboard. Already distortion made the light around it a thin halo, getting thinner as they got nearer. He shook off the crawling sensation in his spine.

"We'll be out of it before capture. Still, take readings. Might learn something useful."

"Of course. Coming to the bottom of the swarl." The ship bucked under the tug-of-war between the black hole's gravity and that of the gravity well.

He forgot his fears, forgot the corona, forgot Scarlet. His fingers moved along the stream, feeling out the paths of least resistance. His toes curled against the deck, seeking purchase against the subtle shifts. He called out orders, not needing acknowledgements, trusting Santiago to comply and sensing each course change in his body along with the adrenaline that made him feel truly alive.

He saw a shadow among the flashing, flowing colors.

"There she is!"

He closed his fist, preparing the capture beam. His hand tingled, the signal that Santiago was also connected to the beam control. They could not afford to miss.

The shadow moved closer. He could only catch teasing glimpses of it in the matter stream. It had to be huge.

"Snag her as we pass. Don't give this swarl any chance to yank her from our grasp. Ready... Now!" He flung his arm toward the ship.

A silver beam flowed from his arm and smacked against the shadow. He waited a tense moment to see if it held. His fist clenched, preparing to fire the beam again just in case.

"We have capture," Santiago confirmed.

"Ha!" he shouted. "Got you, you beautiful thing. Oh, what secrets you'll tell us! Santiago, full ahead. Get us home."

"Dex," Santiago said.

Dex twisted his shoulders and shuffled his feet in a victory dance. "Did you see, Scarlet? How perfect a capture was that?"

"Dex."

He threw his arms wide, embracing the nav field. "You beautiful Disk. *Pageant of destruction/deifier of physics/mad wilderness of the cosmos—*"

"Dex! The ship has powered up."

"What?" With a fling of his arms and quick motions of his hands, he focused on the captured ship. "Let me hear it!"

Among the squeals and buzzing of the Disk, he caught the call of a Civilization B ship.

"Respond back. Maybe it will think we're rescue."

"I've tried. It's pulling away."

His hands traced a path closer to the gravity swirl. "Let's use the stream against it. Oh, how long as it been since we've had a fighter, Santiago?"

Under his feet, he felt the buffeting of the matter stream against the ship.

"I can't hold course."

"Deploy the Mag Net. Let's try to change its vector."

The curling flow of matter left them. With a lurch, they found themselves out of the swarl and the Zone itself and back in the main rush of the Disk.

"Results inconclusive. We're being pulled deeper into the matter stream. Navigation is getting muddled."

"Just hang on. It can't have much power left. Stay in this stream; we'll find a swarl to carry us out once it's given up the fight. And take readings and transmit them! Scarlet, do you see it? Isn't it amazing? We just need to give it time, Molly, time to show it who's boss. Sometimes, that's what hunting is about—patience, endurance, and remembering you're the predator. Molly?"

"*Dex, stay focused!* It's pulling us closer to the black hole." Santiago's artificial voice strained in a way no programmed emotion should.

He shook himself, casting off the phantoms of his family and crew, and glanced to his right. The light around the dark circle seemed a fraction thinner. He hissed through his teeth and turned back to the nav field. He saw a thickness in the stream and pointed to it.

"Resist. See that photon cluster? Get in it. If it wants a fight, it can fight that, too."

Soon he was surrounded by a burnt orange field, the ship lost from view, only the silver line beside him showing they still had it.

A laugh escaped his throat. "Got some spunk, doesn't it, Scarlet? Oh, I wish you were here."

"Dex, pay attention!" Santiago urged, his volume increasing. "It's helping...but the ship is trying to pull ahead and drag us out."

The beam had moved from his side to his eleven o'clock position. He growled, feral and gleeful.

"I didn't want to do this, but it's us or you, and you are too worthy a prize to give up now. Santiago, shock beam. Try to disable it."

He watched as brilliant pulses traveled down the beam, but the ship's vector didn't change.

An alien screech made him slam his hands to his ears before Santiago could mute it.

"Ineffective. I think we made it mad." Santiago sounded more tense than sardonic.

The cloud around Dex thinned. He pointed to a cluster of swirling spacetime.

"Increase speed. Get us in that clockwork of swarls. We'll ride the currents up. It can't resist that." The ship shook, making Dex stagger.

"I don't think we can get there."

"I'm not giving you up," Dex muttered through bared teeth. "You are a fighter, and like nothing in recorded history..."

Around him, light reddened

"We're getting pulled under the corona."

"Aim for the swarl! We are bringing it out of this tangled hell and into the cleanness of space, whether it wants to go or not."

"I don't have the power, Dex. We have to let it go."

"No! Get us to that swarl. Take this current!" He shoved his flattened hand port, felt the ship rock, but not enough. His right side ached. He risked a glance and saw the light starting to dome around them.

"I've missed it," Santiago said. "Event horizon approaching. Spaghettification shields at maximum. It's not enough. Dex, *we have to let go.*"

"No! We'll take this ship or die trying."

"That might be exactly what happens!"

He felt the strain of the shield in his own body as the severe bending of spacetime tried to pull him long and thin, like spaghetti through Scarlet's beautiful puckered lips. "Drag the beam in. All engines port. Shock beams."

"Insufficient," Santiago's voice sounded slow and distorted. "Unable to release..."

Pain threatened to drive Dex to his knees. He glanced portside, toward the control console and saw the holographic black hole growing, the lights around it thinning and distorting, becoming streaks. "Santiago," he gasped.

The control panel itself had started to distort, pulling and narrowing as the gaping maw of darkness grew larger.

A sudden instinct made him fling himself portside.

The universe flared brilliant white before darkness overtook him.

CHAPTER THREE

The night on Squatty Mountain was cool for the time of year, but a campfire brought warmth and merry brightness as Dex's father added another log. A slight breeze played through the pines, making a soothing rustle. In the distance, a pack of helden called to each other on the hunt.

Fifteen-year-old Dex Hollister noted the sounds, then, deciding they were too far to be a concern, returned to the book he was reading.

Dex's father reached over and snatched the datapad from his son's hands.

"Hey!" Dex jerked back to reality and blinked at his father as much in surprise as to readjust to the dimmer light around him.

Vaughn Hollister squinted at the readout. "Physics again?"

"Yes, sir." Dex lowered his gaze to the fire but turned away quickly because he was destroying his night vision; then he realized staring at the datapad had pretty much done that, anyway.

"This for school?" his father asked instead of scolding.

Dex squirmed nonetheless. "No, sir."

Rather than the lecture he expected, his father handed him back the datapad. "This what you want to do, then, instead of the hunt?"

Dex knew he was talking about something larger than reading the book versus their camping trip. "Can't I do both?"

His father pursed his lips. They sat in silence, but he didn't dare turn back to his book, not while his father looked like he had more to say. The elder Hollister poked at the fire with a stick. The snapping embers seemed unusually loud. Dex, in turn, poked at the dirt with the toe of one boot and tried not to fidget. He kept his gaze firmly in the darkest spot of the forest behind his father until he could make out the shapes of the mossy trees in the shadows.

Finally, his father sat back and looked him square in the face. With his vision readjusted to the darkness, Dex saw the whites of his father's eyes, almost supernaturally brilliant against the stark brown irises. He rubbed at his beard. Was he nervous or thinking?

"How you going to do that?" his father asked.

Dex shrugged. "Do I have to know now?"

He half-expected his father to rise, head shaking, and retire to his tent, letting silence express his disdain. To his surprise, his father laughed.

"No, son, I guess you don't. Might be the perfect opportunity will present itself, and you'd best be prepared." Sighing, he slapped his hands on his knees and stood. "For now, though, we'd best prepare this camp. Those helden might be a mile or two off, but whatever they're stalking's bound to get desperate, and you never know what a desperate prey will do."

Have you always wanted everything? An alien, female voice intruded into his memory, speaking in silken tones. *Come to me. I offer you that and more.*

* * *

"Dex," Scarlet whispered, her voice tinged with worry. "Dex, please wake up. Something's wrong."

Dex groaned in protest, squeezing his eyes shut. Yesterday had been a hard day. His body ached, and his head pounded. A few more hours...

"Please, Dex. You have to wake up." Her voice cracked with fear.

Dex forced himself to wakefulness. For Scarlet.

He was lying on the floor of the hallway, twisted into a fetal position facing the control room. The floor felt warm in spots. Why would it be warm?

"Scarlet?"

He blinked, the scene resolving into a partial focus. The emergency lights cast a dim glow on the blue haze, accented by the occasional strobing of the regular lights or the spark of a console. Everything smelled of ozone and melting plastic. Loose equipment scattered across the floor; his roller chair had wedged itself under the console. He tilted his head up enough to see the console itself; torn wires poked out of the casings, as if the console had been torn in two, then the pieces shoved roughly yet perfectly back together.

"Scarlet!" Heart thundering, he took a breath to call louder, but smoke filled his lungs. Sometime during his coughing fit, he remembered that Scarlet had died years ago. Ten? Twenty? Didn't matter. It was just him and...and...

"Santiago?" The ship's name came back with difficulty, but once he had that, the rest of his memories flooded into place. "Santiago, report."

Only silence and the buzz of static replied.

He forced himself up, slowly, stopping when he could sit with his head resting on his hands. Even that effort had cost him, and he waited for the dizziness to pass before calling the ship again. When Santiago didn't reply, he crawled to the adjunct control panel and took out remote control equipment. He adjusted the cap on his head, settled the fingers of the control gloves more firmly into place, and called up the back-up system. He found it functioning and puffed out a sigh of relief. Nonetheless, the outside sensor readings displayed wild, twisted lines of light and energy interspersed with long moments of static or complete blankness. Nonsense.

He turned his attention to the capture beam and laughed when he found their prey still on the other end, surging ahead, pulling them along.

All of that! You nearly killed us, but you're still mine! His laughter set him coughing, but the air in the cabin had started to clear.

Dex set the backup program to run diagnostics and repair on the *Santiago* and pulled off the controls, leaving them hanging from the wall where he could grab them quickly. Then, he bullied his body to stand. His legs ached and his knees felt like jelly; he leaned heavily against the wall as he staggered to the bathroom.

The tepid water felt wonderful on his face and neck, and he splashed himself several times before he noticed how bright the small bathroom was. His eyes flicked to the window, and his body followed until he stood, nose pressed against the glass, awestruck at what he saw.

A thin veneer of blue rays marked the event horizon. Below the horizon, he saw undulating waves of blackish red light fighting to break free of gravitational pull. Above the horizon, curious bows of light streaked yellow and orange.

His breath accelerated as he realized where they were. His memories of the last few minutes before the accident returned.

They'd crossed the event horizon. They were inside the black hole!

He staggered away from the window until he hit the wall and sank down against it. "Santiago! *Santiago!*" He wanted to shout, but his voice came in a hoarse whisper. "Scarlet!"

He clenched his jaw and forced his breathing to slow. The last thing he should do now was panic. He made himself get up and look out the window again, staring hard, trying to notice any changes in the relative size, position or red-shifting of the light around him. He didn't see any.

So, we've crossed the horizon but aren't falling into the hole? He didn't understand how that could be—nor how the spaghettification shield had reasserted itself after nearly failing. Good thing it had, however, or they would have been ripped into quantum elements.

"Not enough data," he growled to himself. "No good planning in a—ha, ha—vacuum. Got to set priorities, then plan."

Priority One: Diagnostics and repair of basic systems. The backup computer was already working on Santiago. Dex shoved himself off the bathroom wall and limped to the medical chair. It felt good to settle into the contoured seat and feel the cushions inflate to support him while the sensors took readings. At the chair's direction, he pulled down the helmet and followed its commands to focus, cough, take a deep breath... He downed a couple of painkillers and rested the back of his head against the cushion while he waited for the results.

No concussion—good. He needed to keep a clear head. Smoke inhalation—expected, but nothing that wouldn't dispel in time. Already the air in the ship looked and smelled cleaner. The chair recommended the scrubber, so he placed the mask over his nose and breathed deeply, allowing the charged air to pull the impurities from his lungs as he read on.

Microtears in the muscles and organs—mostly on the left side. Yeah, he could feel them, all right, but they'd heal. He'd had worse. The hairline stress fracture on his leg could pose a problem. He had a bone knitter, but it would take several sessions to completely heal the wound. He couldn't follow the chair's advice of a cast and bed rest. He'd have to splint it.

He called up navigation.

For the moment, they seemed in stable orbit around the singularity, but that didn't mean it would last. Dokuchaev zones were only theorized, but most agreed they were unstable—and this was no ordinary black hole. He was working against the clock—however that clock might run.

What kind of universe would he return to? Molly would probably be dead, was probably dead already, maybe even of old age. Would she have cursed his folly?

Maybe, he thought warmly, *but she chose this life, too. She knows the risks of relic hunting. More likely, she's cursed me for not fixing up Santiago first—and that she didn't get to say, "I told you so."*

The diagnosis of his spine popped up, and he laughed: the pulling of the singularity as they crossed the event horizon had realigned his vertebrae. Now that he thought about it, his back did feel pretty good. What were the chances?

"Some dive, Dex," he grunted. The three words sent him into a coughing fit, but it helped expel the pollution he'd breathed in. When at last he could catch his breath, he removed the mask and leaned back against the seat as he called for the computer to report on the status of the *Santiago*.

He gritted is teeth as the ship recited the litany of damaged systems.

"It's bad, Scarlet, bad as I've ever been in, but not the worst it could be. I'm alive; the ship is pretty much intact—God knows how. Life support's running. We've still got the ship in our clutches—or it's got us; only time will tell—and we haven't been crushed yet. There's still hope. Question is, how to act on that hope?"

Or maybe the question is, what do I have to act with? he corrected as he set a thin but strong splint on his leg. *I can hobble around here well enough, but all things considered, I should hold off on any external repairs unless absolutely necessary. An EVA is not good on a broken leg.*

He wasn't sure what shape he was in for making internal repairs, for that matter. More and more, he'd come to rely on Santiago's feedback and its holographic projections of the areas he was working on to guide his hands. Now, he didn't have either.

Maybe he shouldn't have turned down Molly's help after all. A Union ship—well, *her* Union ship—might have made the difference; and if not, it would have helped to have some extra hands and supplies.

Supplies! His face broke out into a grin, and with renewed energy, he hobbled to the large supply room beside the airlock where

Santiago had stored the crate she had sent him.

Along the way, he scanned the hallway walls for signs of stress damage and poked his head into the rooms. The main level held the bridge, living areas and part of engineering; most of engineering lay on the deck below. Of course, the gravity generators had to be the one thing that managed to survive unscathed, but he didn't dare change the settings until he had evaluated them. He did not look forward to navigating the ladder with a broken leg. *Handle that when I get to it.*

He ran his hands over the bedroom wall, feeling where a weak point in the metal had caused it to buckle. He'd be lucky to get the door open enough to squeeze through. Across the hall, the walls to the engine room felt smooth as usual. He slid a finger over a grease stain left from some long-forgotten foray into repairs; it was gritty with trapped dust. Scarlet would have been furious.

Hardly matters now, he thought as he wiped his hand on his pant leg. *Curious that the port side got the brunt of the pulling.* He had a vision of the ship being stretched like a rubber band, the pulled side taking the most strain, then snapping back into shape. Had

Santiago fired starboard thrusters to push them toward the event horizon in a last-ditch effort to save himself and Dex? His backup systems lay slightly starboard of the center of the ship and in the mid-level. It was supposed to be the most protected area; Dex found himself wondering about that now.

He resisted the urge to check for himself. The computer had given him its assessment, including a foreboding "indeterminable" when asked how long until it could get his friend online. He wasn't looking forward to the specifics, however. He couldn't see well enough for fine work even if he could see the damage. Better to check what Molly had given him and pray that there was something he could use to get them out of this mess.

He reached the airlock that separated the large and small storage sections from the living areas of the ship, and double-checked that the outer airlock maintained integrity and that air pressure and content were normal. Reassured by the readings, he opened the door and stepped through. The large storage room stood empty, the equipment and cargo bots secure in their closets. No dust and debris here; it was all sucked out into space when the outer doors opened.

Molly used to gripe at the design "flaw" every time they had to tie down a relic too large to move into the small storage room.

"Could be worse. You could have to sweep this room," Dex would say, and she'd laugh. They always swept the ship before a run and set the dirt near the airlock to get sucked out into the Disk if they brought in a captured relic. It was one of their "good luck" rituals.

I should have swept. I didn't sweep before this run. But the ship was too big to bring in, I thought. Why bother? No, I should have swept.

The broom was in the small storage room. He pressed his palm against the door sensor. He'd get the broom, sweep up...

Scarlet's casket sat on the worktable in the center of the room.

Dex gasped and his knees buckled. He clung to the doorway as memories took over.

Standing before Scarlet's casket, caressing her hair, too spent for tears. So tired, so old. He ran his fingers against her cheek, feeling the lesions from the illness that had spread too fast for treatment. Too fast because they'd noticed too late. *He'd* noticed too late.

"I'm sorry, Scarlet," he whispered.

Molly coming behind him, taking his hand. She'd quelled her own tears, trying to be strong for him. He could feel her hand quivering in his.

"Dex." Even Santiago spoke with a hush. "We're under the corona now. There's a calm approaching. If we launch in the next five to seven minutes, we can send Scarlet straight into the event horizon."

He wanted to scream. He wanted to curse the ship, curse himself. He wanted to crawl into the casket—really a standard shipping crate—wrap his arms around his dead love and tell Santiago to send them both into oblivion. But Molly's hand trembled in his, and Scarlet had been a second mother as well as a friend to her.

His voice rasped, "Do it."

He'd climbed the Keirom Cliffs, hunted the warblers, mapped the Zone, captured relics of ancient civilizations...but pulling his hand away from Scarlet's hair was the hardest thing he'd ever done.

As the cargo bot secured the lid into place, Santiago recited passages from the single book to survive humankind's millennia of growth. Some of the words had lost their meaning, but the comfort they offered remained the same.

Ashes to ashes, dust to dust...

Dex forced himself to stand and stagger to the casket that had impossibly returned to his hold. It could not be! They'd sent it into the black hole—the memory shredded his heart as surely as the tidal forces should have—*had!*—shredded her corpse. So how... why...

A cargo bot, responding to his presence, disengaged from its charging section and moved to the crate.

"No!" The word caught in his throat, strangling him.

The bot, unheeding, grasped the lid.

Dex lunged forward to throw himself over the casket.

Then he saw the identification numbers and symbols for the *Blaze*. Molly's ship. It was a crate—just a crate. 2.3m x 1m x 1m. Standard shipping crate. The memories released him, but left a sick knot in his stomach, and he snarled at himself for being such a fool. He wiped his streaming eyes, cursed the smoke that the air scrubbers had long since cleared out, and approached.

The bot pulled a stool to him, and he perched on it as he peered into the box. Nestled in the packing foam were several things he recognized and blessed Molly for: Two repair microbots—perfect for rewiring the ripped control console—and a case of dawlsu. He tore open one bag and breathed in the sweet, spicy aroma. His stomach growled, and for the first time in days, he looked forward to a meal. He saw the message light blinking on the side of the crate and pressed the button to listen to the recording while he ate from the bag with his fingers.

A head-and-shoulder hologram of Molly hovered over the crate. "Hey, Dex. Let me guess: at this moment you're eating dawlsu with your hands? I put some napkins in the crate."

He didn't bother to check. Molly looked good in the blue Union uniform. Captain's stripes suited her. So tall and confident— quite a change from the tangled-haired dockrat with the defensive crouch who had latched onto him and begged for a chance. He and Scarlet had apprenticed several hunters—Daniel, Kixek, Hilde, Xan and...

Who was the straw-haired guy? Attracted more chaos than the Disk; hadn't lasted one run before I set him on cleaning duty for all our safety until we could dump him back on Keldar. Still. Molly had outshone them all.

He'd lost track of what she was saying, but the tone had been scolding. "...so since you won't go take care of your eyes, I found you the next best thing. Go ahead and open the blue case."

Acceding to the tyranny of his former apprentice, he wiped his hands on the moistened cloth he'd found in the crate, as promised, and opened the small case. He chuckled. How long had it been since he'd seen a pair of these?

"They're spectacles, Dex."

"I know what they are," he growled. He turned them over in his hands, bemused.

"Be careful with those lenses. There are nanites in the glass. They'll pick up your focal point and adjust the thickness accordingly. They're kinetically powered, so if things start getting blurry, just take them off and wave them a few times."

"I know, Girl," he replied as he waved the glasses in small circles. *Butcher—Dr. Chap Butcher! He'd had a pair. Made it look like his eyes changed size every time he focused on a different part of the classroom. Gave me the creeps.*

He stuck the spectacles back in their case but shoved the case into a pocket of his pants, nonetheless. No one was going to see him, and they would come in handy.

Molly had finished her spiel about the specs and moved on to the data cores. "These are as much for Santiago as you. Remember my friend Xel Pontia? The linguist at Keldar?"

She blushed as she said his name. More than a friend, then. No wonder she was so interested in the First Contact missions with the Elomijans.

"Well, he's got this theory that the Elomijans are somehow related to Civilization B. Apparently, they have a legend that they are the descendants of a race whose homeworld was destroyed by war not long after they'd started their colony on Elomija. So he's been analyzing the relic transmissions against the Elomijan language—and he's finding similarities. How exciting is that? He's trying to build a comparative dictionary—Civilization B to Elomijan to Human. He's asked me to see what Union ships would like to participate, and I know how much you've ached for a Rosetta stone, Dex. You never thought the transmissions were as simple as identification sequences. And Santiago likes a good puzzle.

So this is a copy of Xel's research so far. The two of you can play with it and let me know if you come up with anything."

The hologram shrugged, but Dex caught the smile. She was hoping he'd come up with something so she could impress her "friend."

"We can't let her down, can we, Santiago?" he asked.

Silence answered.

CHAPTER FOUR

Dex sighed. "Computer, how long until the AI is back online?".

"Unable to determine," the mechanical voice replied. The feminine tones sounded wrong to his ears.

"Can the AI be repaired?" he demanded. His heart clutched, but he had to know the worst.

"Unknown at this time."

"Can it be partially restored?"

"Unknown at this time."

Dex growled between lips pressed tight. "How long until you can tell me?"

"Unable to determine."

He leaned his head against the cool metal of the crate and recited Lepto's Last Canon until he felt his blood pressure lowering. "AI repair is top priority after Life Support," he told the computer.

"The shield generator sustained minor damage that could become critical if kept under current stress," the computer warned.

He folded the bag of dawlsu and pressed the edges to reseal it. No wasting food; who knew how long he'd be here? As he wiped his hands, he told the computer to comply with his command. Then he gave instructions to the cargo bot to secure the items in the crate and play the data disks. After all, he didn't have the computing power of Santiago, but he had good ears.

Finally, he snagged one repair bot and hobbled to engineering and the generator. Looks like he'd need those glasses after all.

As expected, his leg responded to the stress of descending the ladder with sharp jabs of protest. He paused at the base of the ladder and surveyed the engine room, grateful to see nothing on fire, nor the belching smoke, spitting sparks, or the split-apart-and-shoved-back-together look of the bridge. Red lights warned of damaged systems. He gave them a cursory glance to confirm what the computer had already told him before heading to his first objective, the shield generators.

The two machines sat side by side, the bulky human one dwarfing the sleek alien one. Their harmonizing purr had warped into angry growls, but both were still working well enough to fight off the gravitational pulls of the black hole and keep the ship from ripping apart on a string level. Even though Dex felt sure that their survival depended more on the alien shielding, he went to the human one first. Better to tackle the one he knew best.

Dex hissed with pain as he knelt to get level with the generator. His foot spasmed, and suddenly, he was fourteen years old, his ankle wrapped in sticks and torn clothing, making his agonizing trek down Squatty Mountain while his father urged him on.

"No!" he grunted, fighting as the memory, the pain, the fear, all threatened to take over his consciousness. "Not now, dammit!"

He felt the tickle on his wrist, and the confusion waned as his bracelet fed him medications through his skin. Only a few moments had passed. He'd gotten lucky this time.

Shaking his head and ignoring his leg, he slid his spectacles on. The world flew into focus, making him forget his discomfort. He rubbed his chin, bemused. He'd forgotten how things looked with sharp edges. He undid the two screws holding the metal panel in place and set it aside. Again, the glasses surprised him; as he peered into the tangle of wiring and circuits, the magnification changed. He concentrated hard on a circuit and was rewarded by seeing the crisscrossing pattern of the monofilaments. He laughed but resisted the temptation to play. Instead, he willed his eyes to a wider view. Some burned-out circuits, a couple of tripped breakers, scoring along the resonator...looked like friction burns rather than sparking... Santiago had pushed the system beyond its limits, and it had pulled through. Scarlet would have been proud. With some careful planning and the help of his repair bot, he wouldn't even need to take it offline.

He patted the casing. "Good girl."

He completed his triage of the damaged generator, programmed the new repair bot to assist, called for his older, clumsier bot to bring supplies, and got to work. With the repair bot handling the simpler tasks of replacing parts and repairing damage in hard-to-reach areas, he started bypassing circuits that could not be easily fixed. His hands moved with the ease of familiarity. It wasn't the first time he'd kludged a work-around until he could get back to a base and do a proper repair job. He hoped it wouldn't be the last.

The recordings of the Elomijan language kept him company as he worked. He couldn't shake the feeling that the accent of the alien language was somehow familiar, and that he would recognize it if the voice were female. The familiarity tickled against his ear like breath: *Don't you want to know who I am?*

"Go away! I have a ship to fix!"

The computer paused its conjugations. "Please restate the command."

"Never mind. Keep playing."

Two hours later, when he reattached the panel, he discovered he couldn't stand. While his mind had been absorbed in the complexity of repairs, his body had endured in silence. Now, it would take no more.

With a moan, he surrendered and lowered himself gently to a sitting, then prone, position. He eased his legs straight, then spread his arms as best he could in the narrow area. He relaxed, breathing deeply and slowly, acknowledging his weariness without letting it overwhelm him. Instead, he focused on his breaths, in through the nose, out through the mouth, feeling the air move into his lungs, imagining the oxygen entering his bloodstream. He concentrated until he imagined feeling his blood coursing through his body, encouraging each cell to buck up and get to work. As his energy returned, he raised his torso until he was sitting, then continued forward until he bent over his knees, feeling the stretch along hamstrings and spine. On a good day, he could still touch his toes.

"Today is not that good of a day," he said aloud. Instead, he sat back up and called for his bot to fetch him some water and a pain killer. While he waited, he did a few more stretches, shoulders and arms, careful of the torn muscles and injured leg. He demanded an update on repairs to Santiago and again got a litany of Unknown, Unknown, Unable to Determine. His calf itched, so he removed the splint and scratched. Such a sweet feeling, just to scratch—the gentle relief of nails scraping on skin. Even after he'd chased the itch away, he continued to scratch, letting the motion lull him until the bot returned.

He slapped the pain patch on the carotid artery, the quicker to send the medication to his bloodstream, then swallowed some water and tucked the bottle into the leg pocket of his pants. He did a few more breathing exercises, faster to better build his energy. Kixek had taught him those, what, thirty years ago?

"You're old, Dex," he told himself, "but you ain't dead yet."

Suddenly, fury burned red-hot in his body. He twisted his head back toward the computer that stored the AI and yelled, "You hear me, Santiago? I ain't dead yet, and if you don't get yourself back online and I die, it's on your circuits. Yours! You hear me?"

He paused to catch his breath. "Thank you," he whispered. "Thank you for saving my life. Now get operational so we can get out of here."

"Estimate on repairs now possible," the computer answered.

"I don't want to hear it," he growled. "Shut up and keep working."

He slid over to the second generator to follow his own advice.

The casing of the alien generator had an iridescent glow, and no one had ever figured out if it was designed that way or some fluke of the metal made it shine like the otherworldly thing it was. Nonetheless, it was a pretty little jewel in the stark and crowded engine room. It had been even prettier when he'd first salvaged it from a Civilization B drone some thirty-eight years ago.

At the moment, however, it languished under a thin film the smoke had left behind, and it grumbled. He recognized the gravely crunching—he'd blown that piece of machinery more than once on a run—but the low whine was new, and he had no idea what it meant.

For thirty-four years, he'd worked under the assumption that he didn't need to know the theory behind why it worked or even why it functioned the way it did. He just needed to understand it enough to recognize a broken part and replace it.

He removed the protective case, wiped the soot off his hands. and started methodically checking and replacing parts.

Scarlet had been hesitant about his mission to adapt it to a human ship, and he'd teased her about not wanting him to ruin its pretty shell.

"Who cares about that," she'd retorted. "I don't want you to blow up our home!"

She had been right, of course. They'd been spending half their time on Keldar doing research, and half on hunting missions for the university—until he blew up the university ship while on a test run to power the device. Fortunately, they'd sent it out alone, controlling it remotely, so no one was killed for his foolishness, but he'd pulled every string he had with the university to fund the project, and they were not only out an artifact, but a research vessel. He'd lost his job and had come home expecting to lose his wife, too.

Instead, she'd fed him and rubbed his back while he ranted. When he'd at last gotten the sting of losing his job out of his system, she left him alone to study the data from the explosion, bringing him meals to his study and rubbing his shoulders, but otherwise leaving him alone for the next two weeks.

And when he schlepped into the kitchen and announced that he was baffled, she'd slid him the data disk with her own conclusions and design suggestions, then left him alone to digest it. Four hours later, he'd run into the living room where she'd been reading, swept her out of her seat, and swung her around. An hour afterward, they lay in bed making plans. They'd need a new relic and a better ship. He'd started calling in favors while she contacted her father.

The Danes' reputation for shipbuilding spanned three systems, but even they were hard put by Dex's and Scarlet's requirements. The shell itself was standard enough, as were many of the systems. But the AI...

"Dex!" Scarlet's cousin Kristie had thrown up her hands after he'd rejected their fifth program. "You're asking the impossible! We are not going to be able to design an AI that understands Civilization B."

"I'm not asking you to. It doesn't have to understand the language or how it thinks. It has to adapt. It has to find other ways to communicate until it learns its language—or the device learns ours. Look, the drones have their own intelligence. I'm sure of it. We'd managed to bend the CivB shielding device to our will, but the university AI couldn't force it to work on its own, and it didn't know how to react when the device failed to comply. Our AI has got to have finesse. It's got to..." He broke off with a snarl of frustration.

Suddenly, Scarlet was behind him, running her hands over his tense shoulders, rocking him slightly. "Tame its moods?" she quipped, and he smiled and patted her hand.

As Kristie watched them, a smile grew on her face. "You don't want a control system. You want it to be a lover!"

Six months later, Dex and Scarlet, with Daniel Montague, their first apprentice hunter, set off to find a relic in their new ship, the *Santiago*.

"Is that what it is? Are you lonely?" Dex asked the shield generator as he removed another burned out...something...and replaced it with a new one. He'd already had to skip over some broken pieces because he lacked replacements. He prayed that they wouldn't need them. "Computer, analyze the hum coming from the alien shield generator. Compare it to Civilization B drone language."

"To comply would require 25 to 40 percent of current computing power," the program responded. "Shall I continue?"

He huffed a sigh. "No. Continue to devote all possible energies to repair the AI. But keep monitoring the tone and inform me if it changes. Sorry, baby. We'll both have to wait this out."

A few more replacements, and he'd done all he could without Santiago to talk him through the intricacies of the system it now understood better than he did. *I got lazy; started depending too much on my ship.*

His legs quaked when he stood, and even with the pain patch, he could feel the ache. His arms felt like lead, and a blister had formed on the back of his hand from where a spark had caused him to jerk and bump it against a hot pipe. Now that he was no longer concentrating on the generators, he was acutely aware of the unnatural pressure behind his ears from the spectacles.

He tried not to think about it as he moved on to his next objective—the command console. As he passed his bedroom with its buckled wall, he gave the door an experimental push. It gave about three inches, just enough for him to get a depressing peek at the carnage that had been his few prized possessions.

What he saw when he reentered the bridge almost drove him to his knees.

The cargo bot, obeying the commands he'd given earlier, had pulled the broken console apart. Wires dangled. The detritus of broken computer parts littered the space between the two halves, some warped by their experience.

He staggered to the chair, now tucked neatly to one side, and collapsed into it, staring at the wreckage, too stunned to curse. The spectacles focused on every damaged item in too-startling clarity. He pulled them off. The world went soft. He longed for his bed, but the thought of trying to muscle the door open made him ache.

I could drag the crate off the table. His eyelids drooped as he imagined himself nestled snug and warm in the packing. To close his eyes and let sleep take him until death did.

He jerked himself awake with a curse. What was he thinking? He was alive enough to hurt, the ship was basically intact, repairs were underway—and they had caught the relic ship. Even crossing the event horizon, it could not lose them. He couldn't just throw their victory away.

"Computer!" he called out. "You have an estimate on repair for the AI?"

"Affirmative. AI should be online in nine hours, twenty minutes."

"Estimate for extent of damage to AI program itself?"

"Unknown until after initial reboot."

"Take what you can get, Dex," he muttered and sighed. He reached into the side pouch of his chair and found that the energy bars Santiago had insisted he pack were still there. "Computer, start a fresh pot of coffee, strong. And show me a schematic of the command console. Just hang on, Santiago.

We're in the airlock, but we're not in the vacuum yet."

He ate and drank only long enough to study and categorize the problems with the console. The mess was a swarl in and of itself. The bots might be able to handle it, but not without Dex's direction. If only Santiago were running!

No help for it. He made a plan and issued commands to the bots, then got started on his own work.

It wasn't long before fatigue made Dex's hands tremble so much that he could hardly hold a tool. His vision grew so blurry not even his fancy spectacles could compensate, but at least he had a conquered the worst of the damage. He could let the repair bots continue the work while he rested.

He stretched out on the hard deck, willing his muscles to relax. The cold seeped into his skin, magnifying his discomfort instead of numbing his pain. The shivers distracted him from sleep.

"Computer," he growled, "play some of those files about the Elomijans."

"The files are broken into sections: introduction and history, dictionary, and legends pertaining to the Disk."

"Legends. I could use a good story." He shifted, trying to ease the pressure against his shoulder blades.

"Playing: Legends of the Elomijans That May Pertain to the Disk. *Elomij and Hudon Quarrel on the Bloody Road.*"

Dex closed his eyes and let the cultured voice of Molly's linguist lull him away from the present.

The war waged on.

It was too late to wonder why. Too many generations had been born, fought and died in the battle against the Worthy Foe. Still they attacked, and still we fought, and the bards sang of the glorious battles and the gods welcomed the courageous heroes. So it had been. So it was. So it would be.

Hudon, god of violence, and his consort, comely Elomij, goddess of beauty and change, walked the paths of the time. Coming upon the Bloody Road, they witnessed the battles—the courage and skill on both sides—and it pleased them. So they walked on further into the future. Each generation of the war thrilled Hudon. Even the machine battles fired his blood, and he admired the cunning of the People. But Elomij grew bored and suggested they find a different path.

Hudon refused. They quarreled. Hudon, already filled with bloodlust from the road and its visions, struck her and sought to take her, but she ran into the past, then hid herself in the murky Might-Have-Been. Hudon cursed her timidity and went off alone into the future to seek a new consort.

When she could no longer hear his raging, she stepped onto the paths and saw that she was not far into the People's future. She wanted to change the path, to thwart her consort, if only to prove to him she was neither timid nor weak. The path, however, flowed too strong and the past pushed too firmly into the future. And yet...

Elomij saw upon the edge of the path a small bump covered in cowardice and obscured by disdain. She recognized now the place where Hudon had kicked his foot, and realized he'd meant to hide it from her. She quelled her anger lest her hot breath destroy what she so dearly wanted to see, and blew gentle and cool upon the bump in the Bloody Road. The cowardice proved mere dust and flowed into the Might-Have-Been, and she smiled upon a new breed of the People.

Thus Elomij discovered the Explorers. They amused her, and she admired their spirit, for they not only sought to change their destiny, but to do it despite the disdain of the People. She had just experienced disdain at the hands of her consort, so she felt kinship for the Explorers and determined to make them her people. She vowed to care for them as a mother and guide them as a teacher. Together, they would make a new path into the Might-Have-Been.

Again, that feeling of familiarity took him, along with a sudden conviction that the story would be key to his survival. There was a mystery here, trapped between legend and reality...

Fatigue won out. As Elomij made herself small in order to speak with the Explorers, Dex's eyes drooped as he finally gave in to sleep.

CHAPTER FIVE

Dex stood on a broad lane thick with blood. Where the lane ended, only nebula-like skies showed. What would happen if he stepped off the path—would he fall forever, or were the starry skies mere illusion? He didn't care to find out just yet.

Two strangers in brilliant, shining clothes strolled arm-in-arm toward him. As they got closer, he realized it wasn't just their clothing that shone. Hair, skin, eyes—all had an otherworldly glow. A primitive part of him had the urge to fall to his knees, but his rational mind made him stand his ground. These were not his gods.

Nonetheless, his heart hammered in his chest when they neared and paused to regard him. The man wore armor of absolute black and his glow came from the bending of the light around it, like the thin glow around the event horizon. He had a hard face and steely eyes. Dex felt the judgment in the god's gaze and threw back his shoulders and jutted his chin in response. The other being, a woman, grinned.

"Who and what are you?" Hudon demanded.

"Dex Hollister. I am a hunter."

Hudon nodded, but whether acknowledging his answer or approving of his courage, Dex didn't know. "You have hunted many of the Worthy Foe."

"Hunted and captured—and many of the People as well."

Hudon raised a brow. "There is a difference?"

He again looked Dex over, assessing, and shrugged. "You capture and sell. You are a merchant."

"A hunter!"

The god flicked a hand, dismissing his correction. "This is of no interest to me." He gave his consort a nod, then continued alone on the trail, bumping Dex with his shoulder as he passed. Dex glared at his retreating path but could not pursue. His feet had stuck in the congealing blood of the path.

"Why 'hunting'?" the goddess asked.

As he turned to answer, the scene changed, and Scarlet had asked him the question as they hid behind a large formation of boulders and branches on Squatty Mountain; he was twenty again and so in love he could feel it in his pores and in the coursing of his blood. The breeze blew wisps of her hair over her face. He clenched his hands against the urge to brush them back. If he touched her now, he'd kiss her, and it wasn't time yet. He needed to know she understood him. He knew himself well enough to know that life with him wouldn't be easy. He needed a woman up to the challenge of Dex Hollister.

So, he turned around and peeked over the rock at the warblers. Adults, mostly males, lounged on cliff tops, idle but alert, while in the caves, mothers attended the young. The adolescents had started a raucous game of tag, diving and swirling amongst each other, trying to see how close they could get without letting another touch them. None had noticed their presence; or if they had, had decided to wait and see if the humans proved a threat.

He motioned for Scarlet to join him, but she was already beside him, her hands resting on the boulder, chin on her hands. "They're amazing," she said.

"Intelligent and cunning. Fierce, too. So, when you go up against a creature like this, it's not just a matter of setting traps. You have to be smarter, more cunning, more stubborn..."

"Sounds like an ego trip." Her smirk took the sting out of her words.

He twisted to face her. "It's not about ego. It's about the challenge and rising to meet that challenge." He started to say more, but she nodded, her gaze again on the warblers, and he fell silent, admiring her profile, the way her lashes dipped and her lips pouted as she pondered his words. He heard a distant, throaty call of the warbler, low and bubbling into the higher registers. A mating call. His heart echoed its desire.

She met his gaze with a steady one of her own, and his heart leapt. Did she sense it?

"So." She drew out the word. "What kind of challenge am I?"

"Depends." He brushed back a strand of hair that had blown across her mouth. "Are you sure you want to be caught?"

"Do you really think the challenge would end there?"

He grinned and caressed her cheek, and it took all his will not to kiss her then.

Again, the scene changed, and he was old and frail, his muscles aching and his bones chilled. His hand pressed lightly against the goddess's cheek.

She smiled at him with kindness that made him want to sing—and to cry. Her mercy encircled him like a cloak, warming him. He shivered and drew it around him, though he didn't know how.

She caressed his cheek. "I wish you good hunting, Dex Hollister. Now return to sleep; you will need your strength and your cunning in your hunt against the People."

* * *

Dex woke up hours later to find a heavy blanket draped over him.

"Elomij?" The dirty air had worked on his lungs and throat so that he croaked the word. He struggled to sit up, hardly noticing his aching muscles as he scanned the damaged bridge. "Elomij?"

"There are no aliens aboard the *Santiago*," the flat computerized voice replied.

"Except for the Civilization B shield generator in Engineering," the familiar voice of Santiago added. "But I do not believe that is what he is talking about. Hello, Dex. Are you feeling all right?"

"Santiago! Are *you* all right?" He pulled the blanket closer, although the voice of his AI comforted him more than the thick fabric. Santiago must have ordered one of the bots to pull it out of storage once he came online. He shivered at the vividness of his dream, though already the memory of it had started to fade. "Santiago, what's your status?"

"I would say roughly equal to yours," the ship's AI replied with reassuring asperity. "Like you, I continue to suffer the effects of the transition through the event horizon. I have shunted basic processing functions to the backup computer in order to maximize my assets where I am most needed. You, however, do not have the luxury of a doppelganger, so I will insist now that you return to the medical chair, accept your medications, then eat and drink."

"One of your most needed assets is to nag me?" He tried to stand, but his entire body protested, and his leg twinged in the splint. He'd overdone it, traipsing around the ship, not that he'd had any choice.

"Without you, we would not have survived. You have done well repairing my systems. Please maintain yourself while I brief you on our situation."

"I think I have a good handle on that already." He called the cargo bot to him and used it to pull himself to his feet, then clung to it as a wave of dizziness hit. After the third deep breath, it subsided, and he made his slow way into the kitchen.

Santiago's voice followed. "Then you are aware that the ship that dragged us in here may be the only thing keeping us from falling into the singularity?"

"Well, don't let go." He leaned against the doorframe of the kitchen and caught his breath before limping to the chair. It held him like a good friend, and he slouched back with a sigh. The bot brought him a steaming cup. His nose twitched. Fresh coffee.

"I don't intend to. However, over the last three hours, I've detected a decrease in energy output from our catch."

"Wearing it down, are we?" Dex grinned into his cup.

"Dex, please pay attention. We need that ship to keep us alive."

He shrugged. *If we die, we die, but I'll take you first.* "How's *our* energy situation?"

"Adequate, but not for long. Having so many systems offline has helped in that regard, ironically enough, but the shields and the capture beam are eating up our reserves."

"Well, let's see what we can do to cut that down. Can you pull the captured ship in?"

"I can attempt to shorten the beam, but whether that will pull it closer to us or us to it is a matter of opinion."

Dex grunted. "Doesn't matter. It will still know we have a hold on it. It hasn't defeated us yet."

"And if it has weapons?"

Dex shook his head. Resting had done more good for him than pain killers and caffeine, and with the help of those, his head felt clear. Like he'd told Scarlet, the challenge of the hunt was understanding his prey. He was starting to get the measure of the alien ship. "We weren't that far from each other in the Disk. It would have used them already. No, it's just as trapped as we are. Can you show me our route for the past ten hours?"

A display of the interior of the black hole appeared before him. Upon a cherry-black canvas, a brilliant stream of light traced a pattern that reminded him of the fanciful, round-petaled daisies Scarlet had painted. He glanced at the faded designs on the kitchen cabinet, then back to the path. Two dark shapes—one, the *Santiago*; the other, the alien ship—followed the path. He smiled with satisfaction as he watched the ship's jinks and twists. "It did its best to throw us, but you held on. Even with all your damage, you held on!" He slapped his thigh.

"It wasn't just trying to lose us," Santiago told him.

The ships froze, and that part of the hologram expanded. Dex saw a smaller object on the path, where they would have come closer had the ship not changed its course.

Dex set his coffee cup on the floor and leaned toward the display. He rubbed his chin. "So, still hiding from the enemy?"

"Unknown," Santiago replied. "It seems to be avoiding everything with equal care." Other blips near the path brightened.

"How good are its sensors compared to ours?"

"That I cannot determine, but I would speculate that considering our ability to capture it and the fact that we have had centuries of experience developing sensor technology that works in the chaos of the accretion Disk, ours are superior. I am also able to pick up and distinguish signals between the ships, yet it seems unable or un-willing to do so."

"My thoughts, too. Well, that's probably in our favor. Both would count us as a threat."

"If we turned off our shield generator and depended on the alien one, we might pass as a part of it."

"What's our prey?"

"Civilization B, but it did react badly to our grappling it, and we do not know what's out there."

"Let's not risk it, then. How is the CivB generator?"

"Functional. Several parts are feeling the strain. I am not sure how long they will last."

"Working against time, then." He rubbed his face, surprised at the sweat and the bris-tle of hair. "All right, bring us alongside. By now, it realizes we're tougher than it thought. It's time it knew we are its master."

"Is that wise? Perhaps we should not dis-turb it."

"We don't have time for timidity."

"Not timidity. Caution."

"Not much time for that, either—but I'll be as careful as I can."

"You? Dex, what do you intend to do?"

"Explore that ship. See if I can find a shield generator, get some spare parts." Despite finding hundreds of relics, they'd never found any that significantly differed from each other in equipment, except between species. His scientific mind marveled at the mystery, while his practical side counted their blessings.

"And if by doing that, we destroy its ability to protect itself?"

Dex shook his head. "If it survived the transition into the black hole intact, then it did so not just once but twice. Ship that size, I'm betting it has backups—and maybe backups to its backups. I'm not going to sit here and passively wait to die. Hey, maybe I'll see an alien. If I'm do end up dead, I can at least go down in history as the first human to see a CivB alien."

"No one will know to record it in history," Santiago retorted, "and you are not funny."

"Do you have a better idea?"

A pause. "I do not. Very well then. What shall I do in your absence? And please prioritize. I am not the ship I once was."

Dex snorted. "You're still twice any Union ship."

"Agreed. Nonetheless..."

He sighed. "Keep watch for dangers and alert me of trouble. Continue repairs. Map the currents; take readings—though if the backup can do it, let it. And Molly sent us some tapes of the Elomij language and culture. They think they might be related to one of the Civilizations. See what you can do as far as translating; might come in handy."

"Anything else?"

Was that exasperation or smugness in Santiago's voice? Dex pushed himself to his feet. "Yeah. Keep the coffee warm."

The cabinets in the near wall of the small storage area by the airlock held what he needed. First, he laid out his suit and instructed one of the bots to double-check its systems. As it ran through the safety inspection, he put the suit belt on to have it handy and opened the cabinet next to the locker. A surveillance bot no larger than his hand went into one of the pouches, the scanner on a Velcro patch on the same side. Next came some general tools: a screwdriver with adapting head, wrench, wire cutters—low tech stuff that worked on anything. The cutting equipment rested on the floor, and he pulled out the tank of liquid cutting putty, checked the hose and nozzle, and set it on the table with the straps facing the edge so he could shrug it on once he'd suited up.

Then he returned to the closet for the most reassuring piece of equipment.

The relic gun felt good in his hands; his confidence grew just holding it. He turned it on its side and checked the charge. Seventy-five percent. Not great, but considering the years it had sat in the closet, unused and un-serviced, not bad at all. Fully charged, the gun could deliver up to seven pulses, each able to knock out a small relic—or knock a human back twenty feet and into a coma. Dex had seen that once, when he shot a man who'd tried to take his money, his gun, and his woman.

A sly smile stole across his face. *And I told the station authorities that I could re-place the money and the gun, but I could search the universe and never find a woman to match my Scarlet. Got banned from the station for twenty years, station-subjective.*

"Worth every one to see her eyes shine," he murmured.

A vision of Scarlet, young and vibrant, teased at his mind. She stood by the suit locker and glared at him with hand on hips and exasperation on her face. "They confiscated your gun and fined us. We ended up losing our money and the weapon, anyway."

Then she laughed, and in the present day, Dex laughed with her and would not explain to Santiago what was so funny.

He ignored the twinge in his leg as he donned the spacesuit. *Go over, set the cutting charges, get ready to run. If the ship doesn't react, enter and explore. Should I send a bot to cut the hull? No, can't afford to lose a bot, and none were programmed for this kind of thing. Any sign of danger, and I'll know how to react; stupid bot would probably keep cutting even as it got blown away.*

"I think you just have something to prove," Scarlet told him.

"Shut up, woman," he snarled.

"Dex?" Santiago asked.

"Not talking to you."

"I see. Have you checked the status of your medical bracelet recently?"

"I'm fine," he replied, exasperated, but directed a bot to bring him a fresh one. Who knew what he might encounter in the alien ship? Better to have a bracelet fully charged with medications.

With the suit on and QC'd, a small tank of cutting putty on his back, and the remote igniter on his belt, he directed Santiago to prepare the airlock.

Santiago had maneuvered so that they were in the sweet spot behind the alien ship, where its wake left a patch of space relatively free of debris and radiation. He assured Dex that there were no dangers from the alien ship's engines, "although I am still unsure about its propulsion process."

"Comforting."

"Perplexing. However, what cosmic activity I'm picking up between us and the ship is of negligible danger to humans—although, at this point, would it matter?"

"Would it?" a female voice added. He couldn't tell if it was Scarlet or Elomij. He told them both to shut up just to be safe.

"Dex? Dex, what color is Scarlet's hair?" Santiago asked.

Is? "Was," he corrected with some heat. "And it was brown, like coffee with cream. You better not have lost all my recordings of her!"

"No. They are safe. Please be careful, Dex. Concentrate on your tasks and talk to me."

What has gotten into that infernal machine? Still, he promised to take care. "Open the airlock door."

Squaring his shoulders, Dex stepped through.

He gasped as he took in the brilliant chaos around him. Light of every color he could name, and many he couldn't, surrounded the ships in lines and flashes that dazzled, a far cry from the simple reds he'd seen earlier.

Where were they? Some sort of interior analog to the Disk? Similar yet different, so different. He had no way of knowing if the light or the ships were moving faster. In the Disk, he sometimes imagined himself like the warblers, seeing and navigating the swarls like they did the air currents. Here, he felt more like the fish they snatched out of the waterfalls—caught helpless along a current he didn't understand and couldn't control. His fate completely outside his hands. He grasped a handhold by the door and shuddered. Yet rather than fear, he felt an overwhelming awe. He rode on the great power of the singularity, the first of his kind ever to see it. Humans had only imagined what went on beyond the event horizon, in the place they called the information well.

"Stuck in the information well, with just a bucket and the hope of a rope." He wanted to laugh, but it seemed sacrilegious somehow. If he could have rubbed his face, he would have. He gave a small grunt—almost a sigh, really—and turned his head away, but the incredible vista lay beneath his feet, too.

"We can still send a bot." Santiago intruded on his thoughts.

He shook himself and heaved in a great breath, letting it out slowly. His breath fogged his faceplate momentarily and bounced back to tickle his nose. He could smell coffee and stale energy bars on his breath. The mundane sensations contrasted sharply with the amazing vista before him.

"No, it's all right. It's just... You're recording all this, right? All spectrums?" He brought a brisk tone to his voice as he reached outside the ship and attached two tow lines, then pulled to make sure they stayed fast.

"Of course. It's a pity you cannot see it beyond the visible spectrum."

Dex nodded, even though Santiago could not see the motion. "Good. When we get out of here, old friend, you can have any upgrades you want. We'll be able to write our own ticket."

"I've recorded that promise as well. Please be careful. I am unsure whether I will be able to escape the back hole alone."

"Yes, Mother. Pushing off now."

The slightest flexing of fingers sent him sailing toward the alien ship. He felt a momentary lightheadedness as he left the *Santiago's* gravity. Scarlet had always told him it was his imagination, but he still believed that growing up on a planet had made him more sensitive to the changes. One thing he knew for sure: his sore bones and muscles enjoyed the freedom from the relentless pull. His pressure suit kept his injuries from tearing open. For a while, he could enjoy the sensation of floating.

It would take him about five minutes to reach its hull, but he resisted the temptation to use his suit's maneuvering jets. One didn't rush up to a wounded animal, and he wanted to keep every advantage he could in case it had another surprise in store. He made regular reports on distances even though Santiago would already know his progress. In return, Santiago confirmed the passivity of the ship.

Even so, a part of his mind wandered into the past and to Scarlet.

Beautiful Scarlet of the coffee-brown hair and the impish smile. He'd only caught a glimpse of her as he'd walked past the bar, but that was enough to make him alter course and set himself beside her.

Turned out, she and her friends had come to see the local Core Man competition, so he signed up, mopped the floor with most of the stationsiders, held his own in the intellectual competition, and completely blew it in the drinking contest. He had to be carried out of the bar.

But Scarlet had done the carrying.

"What have you got to prove?" she'd demanded.

What had I answered? he thought. *Doesn't matter now—come to think of it, didn't then, either. She had the make of me and liked what she saw. That was enough.*

"Five meters," he told Santiago.

With a series of finger movements, he activated the magnets in his gloves and boots just before he got to the hull.

"Contact," he reported.

He paused a minute, then two, the sound of his own breathing heavy in his ears.

"No reaction," Santiago replied after a lifetime. "But be careful. I cannot take readings inside."

He placed a sounding instrument against the ship's hull, took a reading of its depth and the density of the material, then programmed the cutter. As the computer determined the right amount and concentration of acidic compound, Santiago again reported the ship as unresponsive.

Unresponsive? Or biding time? I know you're not dead. Will you welcome your new master or wait in ambush? Dex chewed on his cheek as he started squeezing the compound in a circle large enough to crawl through, but smaller than an airlock. He could always increase the size later. He stepped back, the magnetic boots pulling at his weary legs like the heavy mud of the rain-soaked roads of his childhood home. Warily, he watched as the compound eat away at the hull. If anyone or anything wanted a reason to react, he'd given it.

The last of the compound finished its steady glow, but no force of air pushed the cut-away circle. Had he chosen an airless zone, or had the atmosphere leaked long ago? No matter. He pulled a small, self-propelled scouting bot from his pouch, and then released the magnets of one boot. Gritting his teeth against the pain he knew would come, he stomped on the cut-out as hard as he could.

The circle slid into the interior of the ship and floated.

"No gravity," he reported.

"And no reaction," Santiago added.

The AI held back from expressing his concern, Dex noted. Had his reduced processing power stopped him from projecting terrible scenarios of their impending doom, or had he decided worrying wouldn't help?

Maybe he's decided I can worry enough for both of us.

The acids had stopped burning away at the hull, but nonetheless, he used a tool to test it before going through himself. The last thing he needed was a hole in his spacesuit.

His own light, while powerful, illuminated only a paltry pie-shaped wedge before him. He tossed the spybot down the corridor, and it zipped about, never too far, but enough that its sensors projected an image in Dex's helmet of what lay ahead.

Long aisles of pipes and wires, no consoles, no indicator lights. No knobs. Utilitarian colors—grays of metals, the bland colors of untinted plastics. The floor itself held a pattern of holes of varying sizes. No pictures or symbols, not even anything to indicate deck levels or directions. Dex swore under his breath. He'd been hoping for decoration—in particular, signs with their written language. No such luck yet.

Scanner in one hand, stunner in the other, he moved in.

The floor looked as clean as the first day out of dock, although he did see some scoring that told of shorts and plasma surges. He took a swab out of his belt pouch and ran it across the floor and an unscorched portion of the wall. Nothing.

"This area's cleaner than the room you were made in," he grumped to Santiago.

"No traces of atmosphere, either," the AI added.

He stuck the swab in a vial in case it held some microscopic danger he could not see, and continued. Without atmosphere, he couldn't hear the impact of his boots on the floor, but the pull of the magnetic soles was a comforting normalcy in the barren alien ship. A quick glance at the spybot output showed just more pipes, outlets, and holes. No markings, no lights—nothing that indicated the presence of living beings.

No bodies. With the atmosphere sucked or leaked out, he'd expected a few corpses, but he'd have been happy even with skeletal remains or a pile of dust—anything biological that indicated life had once roamed these aisles.

It's a big ship. Maybe I'm in the engines, then? A stroke of luck, if so; yet he still hadn't seen anything save pipelines and what looked like computer outlets. What he wouldn't give to see some machine parts or a control panel, even a seam to show a panel he could rip off to uncover the secrets of the ship's design.

The spybot reached a dead end, turned and came back. He waited while it sought a new route. *How much of this ship is engine?*

"Santiago, can you tell what kind of atmosphere was in this ship before?"

"I'd have to divert computing resources and deploy another bot to get more readings. Is that a priority now, or are you merely curious? Do keep in mind that our mission is finding a way to repair my systems and get us out of here before we are sucked into the singularity for good."

"Nag, nag. Don't get snappy with me. This place is just too empty for my tastes."

"They may have abandoned ship and put it on autopilot. Perhaps the sample you took earlier might hold some clues. I'll examine it when you return."

A flash of light and static brought his mind back to the spybot, but he didn't see it. It must have rounded a corner. Its transmissions had stopped as well. He replayed the last moments and watched as a squat robot with many arms entered the passageway, paused (he guessed) to send a signal, and receiving no answer, fired upon the spybot, destroying it. Not a security bot, Dex guessed. The laser looked more suited to welding than weaponry. Was it responding to the hull breach? Would it call up other defenses, now that it had seen an invader?

Dex didn't plan on giving it a lot of time. Still, he knew the way behind him was clear, and while getting out alive was his top priority, getting out alive with that bot would be a coup. A few steps from the hull breach, he'd seen a recess. He doused his helmet light and pocketed his scanner, so that he could back up with one hand along the wall to feel for the nook. When he found it, he pressed into it, holding his gun ready, straining his eyes to make out the slightest movement in the dark.

A slight trembling in the flimsy floor telegraphed the machine's approach. All he saw was endless black upon black. He closed his eyes and concentrated on the feeling. His breathing quieted as imagination and instinct showed him the bot's path. Closer, closer. His nerves began to tingle in anticipation. Dainty steps, more like a spider than a beast; his mind imagined a click-click-click. Closer...

Now!

He leapt from his hiding place, headlamp on, and shot at the approaching bot.

The first blast made the spiderlike bot rock, and he had just enough time to note that its legs plugged into holes in the floor before it spun to retreat. He shot it again. The body swung back, though the legs held fast and the arms whirred and jabbed. He wondered if it made a mechanical squeal as well. He fired a third time as it raised its arms toward him, and again before it could fire a laser. The arms drooped.

He shot it once more for good measure, draining the gun, and then grabbed the alien bot and pulled it back to the hole. He dove out first, made a quick scan to confirm nothing outside threatened them despite Santiago's reassurances, then reached back in to nab his prize. This time, he didn't need caution. He braced his feet and pushed off toward Santiago's open airlock. When the airlock doors closed with no sign of retaliation from the ship or the robot, Dex let out the breath he'd been holding.

"Ha! See that, Scarlet? Like when we were young."

Santiago reported full atmosphere, and he removed his helmet. His own robot came out of the small storage area. He instructed it to take his prize away and attach it to an energy drain until they could figure out its power supply and remove it.

While Santiago gave him the run-down on the ship's status and progress on repairs, he went about the business of removing his suit and prepping it for the next walk, then made his own slow way to the kitchen. The adrenaline rush had left him. Weary and achy, he downed a bottle of water before asking about the status of the alien ship.

"It does not seem to have noticed your theft of one of its repair bots, if that's what you're asking," Santiago replied.

"Are you passing judgment? I don't think I like the tone of your voice."

"If by judgment, you mean a moral reasoning, then of course not. However, you went to the other ship to find parts for the CivB generator. I detect nothing appropriate in the hunk of junk you brought back."

Dex guffawed. "Next time, Santiago, next time. I was thinking that 'hunk of junk' might have some schematics or something we can use against the other ship."

"I see. And we shall get this information, how?"

"Not me. You. It's CivB. Sweet talk it the way you do the shield generator."

"I'll try. Incidentally, the ship is replacing the section of hull you cut out and welding it back in place."

"And the grappling lines?"

"Still grappling."

"We've got time, then. You said sensors are online; what about navigation? I'm fine humoring this thing for now, letting it wear itself down pulling us along, but I don't want us at its mercy."

"I have limited abilities, and the holo-nav's human-ship interface is still down."

"That's our next priority, then."

A sudden coughing fit took control of Dex. He braced himself against the wall, pounding one fist as his body racked. It left him with streaming eyes and an aching chest.

"What's wrong with life support?" he wheezed out.

"Life support is functioning within normal parameters," the backup computer intoned.

"Nothing." Santiago verified. "Perhaps it's the suit air and the smoke from earlier working its way out of your lungs."

Dex leaned his head on one arm, still braced on the wall, and panted.

"Dex, the navigation system can wait. Sit in the medical chair. Breathe in some oxygen."

"I'm fine. Just the smoke," he croaked. "I'm not sitting in the chair like an invalid when there's work to be done."

He did, however, bring a canister of oxygen with him. Didn't hurt to be prepared.

Chapter Six

Vaughn Hollister gazed at the wooded landscape through infrared binoculars. After a moment, he grunted. "Yep. There it is. Abandoned by the pack, looks like." He pressed a button on the right-hand side of the binoculars, marking the location, before handing them to Dex. "Wound looks to be healing, but we'd better go slow, just in case. Healing or not, it's still a wounded animal."

Dex focused on the injured breld. The six-hundred-stone mammoth licked the stump that had once been its primary mandible. He grunted his agreement. Even weakened and with one clawed paw missing, a breld could make short work of them if it felt threatened. He scanned the area around the injured beast, the binoculars feeding him wind, temperature and foliage density readings. He clicked a second button on the device and handed it back. "Good spot, just north. Downwind, thick foliage. Go there, tranq it, call for extraction."

"Sounds good, Son."

Together, they started off, not concerned with silence yet. They had a couple of kilometers before they entered the breld's territory. The fern-like branches of the trees drooped, the collected moisture of the morning dew making a steady drip. Birds called to one another, announcing food, advertising for a mate. He heard a scurry of feet to his right; a coonson hunting lizards, most likely. The air was heady with the scent of carnivorous nightflowers putting out a last pheromonal call for prey before folding up for sleep.

"So, you decided? The university?"

Dex pushed aside a fern and let his father go first before answering. "Yeah. Shipbuilding was interesting for a while, but..."

"But you're not a builder. And you weren't meant to be a gamekeeper, either. It's all too small for you. Even this." He waved his arms at the expanse of jungle. "It can't contain you. Sometimes, I wonder that Scarlet is enough for you."

Just her name made his heart grow warm. "Scarlet is different. She knows how to handle me."

His father barked a laugh. "Then she's better than your mother or I."

"You did all right."

His father didn't answer, but pointed to a Lady Lagusa, each hand-sized flower pointing toward them, wide and inviting, its scent promising sweet comfort while its petals pieced the skin and sucked the blood from its willing victim. They gave it a wide berth.

"Had to chase off some poachers the other day, digging up Lagusas. Apparently, there's a growing demand for the plants on the black market. Using them to get space-faced." His father shook his head before returning to their earlier conversation. "I know we did the best we could. It's good that the spouse understands better than the parents. I hope you're giving her the same benefit?"

Dex grinned. "Best part of being with her."

"She okay with leaving her family?"

Dex chewed on his cheek, thinking. "You know, I think there's more of a restless spirit in her than her family realizes. She thinks Lagusas are fascinating. She understands risk. Respects it. We'll be all right."

Ahead, another Lady Lagusa tried to weave its spell over them. They stopped to admire it. This one had petals of interwoven reds, blues, and yellows, narrow lines of color that somehow managed to suggest depth. One could almost imagine touching the lines and discovering they were strings, cashmere threads you could caress like a soft sweater. Dex had the dangerous impulse to grab one of those threads, pluck it, and have it made into a blouse for Scarlet.

"Sometimes, the most beautiful things in life are the deadliest. Why is that?" his father wondered.

Dex shook himself, dismissing the urge but enjoying the thrill it had given him. "Adds to the fun."

His father clapped him on the shoulder. "And that's why the universe won't be able to contain you."

* * *

"Dex."

Santiago's voice drew Dex from his reverie. He blinked at the tangle of red, blue, and yellow wires he'd been staring at. Was that what had made him think of the Lagusas and his father? He'd all but forgotten that day. "What happened to the breld?" Had he forgotten, or had he never known?

"Pardon?"

"Nothing." He pulled himself out from under the console. His leg made its complaint as he tried to find a more comfortable sitting position. It was knitting, slowly, but on its own. *Ha. Told Santiago I didn't need to sit in the medchair.* He pulled off the glasses Molly had gifted him, and the world blurred; a false comfort, as it bathed the damage in soft edges, but a small relief, nonetheless. "Just thinking aloud. You got something?"

"I'm not sure. The alien ship is heading to an area of denser mass and energy."

"A swarl?" Dex stretched, releasing some of the tension in his shoulders from working in the cramped space. His stomach reminded him that he'd skipped at least one meal, and the last thing he'd eaten was an energy bar and a bottle of water.

"Perhaps. What concerns me is it's to port, just as we are."

"Show me?"

"I've only crude holographics through the entertainment console."

"Then it'd better be entertaining." Dex called the repair bot to him and again used it to raise himself up. It was easier than before, he noted with satisfaction. "Speaking of, how goes the seduction of our captured bot?"

Santiago managed to sound affronted. "If by 'seduction,' you mean was I able to communicate with it and gather useful information, I have managed to access some maps, and I think I have identified their engines and shield generator. You are correct; there are several. However, I'm not sure it's cross-compatible with ours."

"That'd be a change. Still, cross that bridge when we get to it."

"Indeed. And the first bridge we must cross is this swarl."

The *Santiago* had two entertainment consoles: one in the kitchen, which doubled as conference room and classroom for apprentices; and one in the bedroom, which Scarlet had insisted on. Dex started for the bedroom, stopped in confusion at the twisted metal of the door. When had this happened? What had they gone through?

"Scarlet!" He tried to shove himself through the narrow opening and lever it wider.

"Dex!" Santiago's voice pierced through the confusion, and he felt a tingle on his wrist. "Dex, concentrate."

"Scarlet?" He couldn't leave her in there alone. She was so sick, and what if she were hurt? "I'm coming. Scarlet!"

"Dex, think," Santiago insisted. "Scarlet is dead. Remember. Concentrate."

Dead?

Lying in bed, holding his hand, so weak until the pain took her and her grip turned vise-like. Part of her face so young, the rest deformed with wrinkles and liver spots, the disease pushing her body to age at two rates. Repeating, "I love you" because it was the only thing they could think to say. The only thing that mattered.

A silver crate with a single blossom of a Lady Lagusa on it.

Pinned between the door's edge and the doorframe, Dex slumped against the door, shaking. Had it not been for the splint holding his leg straight, he'd have sunk to the floor. Dimly, he heard Santiago's reassurances, bringing him back to the present, past the pain, past the grief.

But not past the fear. "How long?" he demanded.

"Only a few minutes. But we're approaching the swarl..."

"Show me." He started to pull himself from between the door and wall. The ship lurched, and he banged his bad knee against the bent door. His leg gave an angry spasm and he cried out in pain. The medical bracelet gave him a boost of pain killer, a weak dose. "Show me!"

"I can't from here. I have tried to put the alien ship between us and the swarl, but it rolls and drags us back into position. I've zapped it through the capture beam. No effect. Course of action?"

"It's going to use the different gravity of the swarl to scrape us off."

"Agreed. What shall I do?"

The painkillers weren't acting fast enough. He'd probably pass out if he tried to get back to the kitchen now. He gritted his teeth while memories of Scarlet toyed with his concentration. Beautiful Scarlet, dying with such ignominy. *Nothing we could do. Nothing I could do.*

"Dex! What shall I do?"

"Hug her. Hug it! Cut the beams. Pull in the grapplers. Get as close to that ship as you can. Keep it between us and that swarl. And whatever you do, don't lose it!"

"Understood. Hold on."

His back against the threshold and arms locked against the edge of the door, he braced himself and waited, blind and helpless, as Santiago fought for their lives. He tried to look out the porthole over their bed, but the swirling colors meant nothing and only added to his confusion. Santiago kept up a steady litany of momentary successes and failures, so he couldn't even call for a status report. His leg screamed for relief; he must have rebroken it.

"How much longer?"

"It's following the swarl. I don't think it will give up."

"Neither will we. Arm another grappler. I want you to target that repaired hole we put in it. If it's going to throw us, we'll take a piece of it with us."

"Coming on target. Firing...and capture."

Again, the *Santiago* jerked and rocked as the other ship tried to escape the beam. Then, everything calmed.

Dex released the breath he was holding. "Well?"

"We are moving away from the swarl."

"Not so sure of your welding, are you?" Dex's laugh ended in a cough. The world around him grayed. He gasped, straining for each breath.

"Dex!"

"I'm fine!" he wheezed. "Deploy more grapplers."

Dex shook his head, trying to clear it. It hurt. Nonetheless, he snarled a second reassurance to the AI as he gingerly extracted himself and limped to the medical chair.

* * *

Hudon's voice echoed in the darkness. "Perhaps not so uninteresting after all."

Dex opened his eyes to find himself sitting on the Bloody Road. He ached everywhere. He examined his arms and legs, found them covered with gashes and bruises. He'd adorned the road with the color of his human blood.

Hudon read his thoughts and laughed. "Poetry as well, hunter?"

He shared the last of his smile to his consort, who smiled in return. Elomij still had an otherworldly beauty, though something had changed. Some of the frivolous air had left her; even her smile held a hint of introspection. Hudon dropped his arm from around her waist.

Dex didn't dare ask what happened, even if his pride would have let him. "What do you want from me?" He braced elbows on knees and rested his head in his hands. He didn't owe these people respect, especially if they had made him fight for their entertainment.

Suddenly, invisible forces pulled him up by the chin and forced his body into a kneeling position. He could only listen, watch, and suffer through the indignity.

Hudon glared, his glow the sullen burning of a red dwarf star. "Be grateful you amuse us, hunter. I have destroyed others for less."

Elomij laid a hand on her consort's arm. "He is not one of ours. Besides, did we not agree?"

Hudon twisted his wrist, and Dex sagged before realizing he had control again. He stood, teeth bared, reveling in the fact that he could seethe and determined to let the god know that he might be able to control him for a while, but he did not *own* him.

Hudon chuckled, as an adult might at a precocious child. So did Elomij, although her smile had a tinge of motherly pride.

"You still haven't told me what you want with me."

Hudon shrugged. "You amuse us. Be grateful. It keeps you alive." With a nod to his consort, he turned and walked a little way down the road, singing, "*How good it is that you and I need not kill the stars and moon. We battle each other, as foes and brothers, and die, oh, much too soon.*"

He paused to lean against a tree that had not been there only a moment before.

With a leisurely air, he scraped at his nails with a dagger. His song faded to low hum.

Elomij took Dex's arm. Warmth spread along it, relaxing muscles and revitalizing him. "We have a game going, and you are doing quite well."

"I don't want to be part of your game."

She beamed at him, as if charmed that he thought he had a choice. "The People have not had an outside foe. You are proving your mettle, and your ship is a worthy weapon. As a prize, I shall give you one hint. You must tear open your prey and retrieve what you need."

He laughed rudely and crossed his arms. "Tell me something I don't know."

Her benevolent smile faded. "What do you mean?"

"This 'game,' or at least the latest round, involved your ship trying to scrape mine off its side like mud off a shoe...or blood." He glanced at the road. "It knew exactly where that swarl was, which means it came from here. If it got out of this time trap once, it can do it again, and I'll make it take the *Santiago* with it."

"You are impressive." Her glow faded to that of a lazy afternoon

"And point of fact," he added, "I have already torn open my worthy foe, and I will do it again and again until I get what I need to get me, my ship, and it back to the other side."

She laughed, a sound like leaves falling from the trees, or the scent of the Lagusa—compelling, beautiful, but not happy. "Why would you want to return? It is no longer the same world."

"It's still mine."

She paused with tilted head. She looked so childlike in her perplexity, he felt his anger melt away. He took her hand.

"Elomij, let me give you a hint. You are not going to like what you find at the end of this road."

"But the road will not end."

"That's even worse."

Her brows knit, bringing a crease to her lovely forehead; then her expression cleared into one of amusement.

"That is a very human attitude, Dex Hollister."

* * *

Dex awoke in the medical chair, muscle-sore and groggy, but without the sharp pains and weariness of earlier. He rubbed his eyes. "How long?"

The computerized voice answered, "You have been undergoing treatment for a fractured tibia, multiple lacerations..."

"Where's Santiago? Santiago!"

"The Santiago system is interfacing with the Civilization B robot retrieved from the alien vessel."

Dex heaved a sigh and tried to calm his pounding heart before the chair administered some meds. "How long has he been doing that?"

"Two hours, fifteen minutes."

Dex swore. Santiago said he'd gotten the layout of the ship. Why was he talking to it? That was either very good or very, very bad. Either way, he didn't want to interrupt the AI. "Status on the alien ship?"

"Still in capture, moving steadily at zero-point-six gips per second toward an unknown destination."

"What was its speed before the swarl encounter?"

"One-point-one-five gips."

He slapped his knee. "Slowing down are we, darling? Let's see if we can discourage you further from such tricks. Computer, prepare the docking tube and run a check on my suit. We've got work to do."

This place is a mess, he thought as he headed to the storage room. The latest fight with the ship had tossed or re-tossed equipment and supplies, so that he had to kick things aside to get through the normally clear hall. Bulkheads that had withstood the worst the Disk could offer had cracked or even buckled; the ship had sealed the smallest storage room because of a hull breach. Some of his loosely screwed-in panels had come open, and the exposed wires showed scoring. He saw no sparks but could still smell the ozone of snapping wires and the welding jobs of the robots. He hadn't gotten very far in the other ship, but he could only hope they'd dealt as much damage as they'd sustained.

Or did he want that? If worst came to worst, could he abandon the Santiago and escape on the alien ship to get picked up by another relic hunter on the other side?

He shook himself, suddenly angry. He and Santiago had been through lots of tight scrapes. Hadn't Santiago just saved his life? No, they'd get out of this alive, the both of them, or die trying. And if they died, they'd take that alien ship with them.

The CivB robot rested in the middle of the large storage area just off the airlock, its arms drooping. Dex circled it, then put on the magnifying specs and examined it again. Like the ship, it lacked what he thought of as the basics: indicator lights, control buttons, even access panels. How did the People fix it? How did they *work* with it for that matter? Were the People blind? But Hudon and Elomij had eyes...

And I know this, how? Stupid dreams. He stopped, rubbed his hand over his face. He needed a shave. And a shower. A long sleep in a comfortable bed. A repair team for Santiago...

He needed to get home—and with the prize that would bring them all that and more.

Mind on the hunt, Dex, he told himself and returned to examining the alien machine. What was Santiago doing with it for two and a half hours, anyway?

Its base rested on the floor, the thin legs angled like a spider's. He crouched and examined one "foot": the rounded column held grooves. He imagined it inserting its foot into one of the holes that dotted the decks, then adjusting to lock in. Probably could climb the walls and ceiling that way, too. It explained the rumbling of the deck. Rather than weight shaking the panels, he'd felt the vibrations of the feet engaging and disengaging.

The sole of the foot was a socket. He remembered that the playback from the damaged spybot had shown the alien machine reaching behind itself before drawing the laser. He'd thought it was just orienting itself, but what if it had the tool on its body and had needed to attach it to the leg? If so, he most likely had a short window of opportunity to shoot a repair bot while it chose something it could use as a weapon. Still better to ambush or sneak past if possible.

The body casing held clips for tools which now waited empty, his own bots having relieved it of anything it could use as a weapon in case Santiago could not control it. In addition, a heavy cable tied it to a bolt in the floor and another, thinner cable to a set of pulleys that would chuck it out the airlock should it get too frisky—all standard for working with an unknown relic. He felt a small relief that his ship had handled the details so well despite the damage to its own systems.

"Computer. Still no sign of swarls ahead?"

"Unable to determine without releasing Capture Beam Three and repositioning the

Santiago. Please state commands to initiate the procedure or assume manual control."

"Never mind. Can Santiago be interrupted?"

"The AI has been informed of your recovery."

"Yet he hasn't bothered to wish me good morning." Dex braced his hands on his knees and stood up, pleased that he could do so without a crutch to lean upon. The time in the medical chair had done him good after all. Unfortunately, if their prey had other bots like this, they would have been repairing it while he was healing. He could not let it gain any advantage.

"Tell the *AI* that I need to talk to him before I go out." He turned his back on the captured alien bot and headed to the small storage area to prep for his attack on the other ship.

Hudon and Elomij might get their amusement, after all. But on his terms.

Chapter Seven

"Good morning, Dex," Santiago's voice filled the small storage area. "What are you singing?"

Dex didn't look up from where he was filling the tank with the cutting putty he'd just mixed. "What?"

"You were singing." The AI replayed a recording of the last few lines: *We battle each other as foes and brothers...*

"If you were listening, why are you asking?"

"Perhaps I should rephrase. The melody bears a striking similarity to an ancient folk song the Elomijan species shared in the recordings Molly gave us. However, I have not played that part of the files for you yet. Where did you hear this song?"

"Is it relevant to our situation?"

"Most likely not."

"Then never mind for now. We've got work to do." If he tried to explain that alien gods had been singing it in a dream, no doubt the AI would send him to his chair or set his own bots after him to wrestle him down and administer a heavy dose of cognitive stabilizers. God—and gods, probably—knew he'd had enough of those already. He set the mixing jug next to the can, and screwed both lids on tightly, listening for the pressure seal. "What have you been up to?"

"What are *you* up to?" the ship countered. "You intended to go outside without my support?"

"If need be." The indicator lights showed green, but he used his new spectacles to double-check the readings. Handy things, these specs Molly had found for him. If she were still alive when he got out, he'd be sure she got a cut of his profits; if not, maybe he could find her heirs—if she'd ever gotten the gumption to tell that professor of hers how she felt.

Relic hunters, especially those that went deep into the Disk, got used to watching their younger friends grow old and die in accelerated leaps while they themselves seemed to follow a steady march of time.

"Relativity is a demon that toys with men's hearts."

"Errin Ovloud, *Disk Dreams*. I do not see the connection."

"Going to be a totally new world when we get back," Dex said as he adjusted the tank so he could shrug into it. He checked the straps and made sure the wand was secure, then pulled his gun out of the charger and attached it, too.

"I will be obsolete," Santiago mused.

"You're never obsolete. Don't get melancholy. Tell me about the captured robot. What the hell were you doing with it for nearly three hours? I was about ready to isolate you from the ship's systems."

"It would have been too late, of course, had it taken over my programming. But rather, I proved the victor. It's a simpler system than our shield generator yet has surprising similarities."

"Tell me later. Right now, I want to know what you did and how it helps us." Everything was prepped, the relic gun recharged. He leaned against the counter to rest before donning the suit.

"I believe I have convinced it that our shield generator is its top priority and have established a communications link to it. I will be able to see through its sensors—"

"Does it see?" He thought about its featureless surface.

"In a manner of speaking, though not as humans do. I will see through its sensors and issue commands to it. We should be able to send it through to scavenge for parts."

Dex pursed his lips, thinking. "Can it jack into the main ship?"

"We were lucky in that this bot is programmed for mechanical repairs and not software, although it does have limited access to the ship's computers. Nevertheless, I do not think I am up to 'romancing' an entire warship."

"We're not taking that chance, anyway. If it tries to jack in, I want you out of its processors and your firewalls set to maximum shielding. Got that?"

"My thoughts exactly, Dex. I'll have the repair bots take it to the airlock and return its tools. What are your plans, then?"

"Wound that ship. This time, when I cut a hole in it, I'm going to bring the piece in with me so it can't repair itself. Might be less likely to play games with variable gravity if its own structural integrity is compromised. I'll attach the docking tube so it has another reason to depend on us."

"An interesting plan."

Dex snorted and left the counter to suit up. "This thing has put up a good fight. A worthy foe, but it's not our brother, and it will know we are its master."

This time, the brilliant and twisting colors didn't surprise Dex, but he paused in admiration, nonetheless. They had long passed the swarl where the ship had tried to scrape them off like some kind of offensive parasite. Too bad. He'd have liked to have seen it with his own eyes. Instead, the lights had settled into a relatively stable streaking of reds in every shade he could imagine. At least as far as he could see; positioned as they were in the wake of the captured ship, their destination remained a mystery. He shrugged off the chill that gave him and set to work.

First, he established a pulley-and-cable system. It would allow him to haul things back and forth, like spare parts the repair robot deemed necessary to fix their own shield generator. It also created another connection between him and the alien ship. Again, he felt a chill. The two were growing interdependent, and he wasn't sure he liked that, even if it was his idea.

As long as it knows who's boss, he told himself, and started laying the cutting putty.

Again, the ship submitted to his surgery docilely enough. He commented on it to Santiago.

"It may not be aware of you," the AI replied. "I cannot find any indication of external hull sensors on the schematics I downloaded from the repair bot."

"You don't think that's a little odd?" Dex double-checked the circle of cutting putty for breaks or bubbles. Satisfied, he maneuvered back to another part of the dead hull and pressed the button to start the process.

"I have few sensors to check for such damage myself, Dex."

"But you have some—and you're not a warship." The metal began to bubble and steam, the smoke immediately sublimating into vacuum. Blink and you'd miss it. Dex didn't often blink, but he did keep an eye on the process—and on the hull, in case Santiago was mistaken and even now, the ship was sending laser-armed robots to remove the offending tick that was digging into its skin.

Once again, however, the ship ignored his cutting into its hull, and he attached a magnetic grappling hook to the circle. This grappler was a small, portable version of the ones Santiago had attached to the ship to augment the capture beams and connected to a reel system inside the airlock. Dex stood back, attached to their prey's hull, while Santiago pulled in the circle. Meanwhile, he debated what to do with the portable airlock. His intention had been to place it over the opening immediately then remove it and take it with him to show that he alone had the power to repair the damage. Without external sensors, however, he wondered if their prey would even notice.

"What kind of warship doesn't have equipment to check hull integrity?"

"Assuming that the system isn't damaged, one that either does not expect its hull to be compromised or one that does not care."

"Neither of which makes sense." He huffed a sigh. Time enough for that mystery later, after he was safe onboard the *Santiago*.

Safe. He almost laughed. "Leave the airlock for now. If it doesn't care, I don't need to. Are you sure about the alien robot? It's going to follow our orders?"

"I'm as sure as humanly possible," Santiago replied.

Meaning, not completely, but enough to reassure Dex—and to leave the decision to his human intuition. "You're not funny. All right, send it over."

For some reason, watching the repair bot inch its slow way from the *Santiago* to the alien ship made Dex dizzy. He closed his eyes against the vertigo, then looked to the side, where the universe—or their small part of it—rushed past them in streaks of auburn. He had the sudden urge to stick his hand outside of the pool of calm Santiago had maneuvered them into. Would it be like sticking his hand out the window of a speeding vehicle, where he'd feel the push of wind? Or like dipping into a rushing stream, where the water swirled around him with cool comfort?

A wave of homesickness overwhelmed him. How long since he had been planetside? Before Scarlet had died.

One does not know the freedom of space/without the pull of a gravitational place.

"One meter, Dex."

He shook himself from his fancy. More likely, he'd have his arm fried by radiation if he extended it past the relative safety of the wake. "*Space deceives; it holds no emptiness/rather its dangers lie hidden/too impersonal for even an ambush.*"

"'Planetside Dreams' by Garron Cor," Santiago said. "Interesting choice, considering our situation. Do you have the robot?"

"Got it." Dex took hold of the bot by one of its repair arms, steadying it as he unhooked it from the line. With a gentle shove, he eased it into the gaping wound of the ship and followed.

Upon finding itself home, it unfolded its spindly legs, inserted them into the holes on the floor, and started down the corridor. Dex followed, cursing the darkness and the need for his helmet light. Master or not, he'd rather have had the option of sneaking around inside the captured ship.

"Dex, use radar," Santiago suggested. "I had your suit modified to use the same frequency as the repair bot. You should be able to pass unnoticed; at least, that signal will not give you away."

He switched to radar, and immediately the world resolved into strobing but clear images as the radar played its results on the face shield of his helmet. He waited for his eyes—and his mind—to adjust to the new way of seeing. "You just now think of telling me this?"

Santiago took on a slightly annoyed tone. "I had expected the secondary computer to inform you, as it did the alterations according to my instructions. It is a most limited partner."

"Not worthy of you, my friend. Maybe we can do something about that when we return to our reality, find you a partner system. Think they'll have created anything that can keep up with you by then?"

"Perhaps we should concentrate on getting back to our reality first," Santiago replied with cool neutrality.

"Right. Don't suppose you found an IFF signal?" If the bots inside the ship had a signal for establishing that they belonged there and he could project it as well, he'd move more easily—and breathe easier, too.

"The only Identification Friend or Foe signals are coming from the ship itself—and even then, not often."

"Too much to hope for." He'd gotten used to the radar images and trusted himself to move on. "Where's our friend?"

"There's a corridor to the right. The way was clear when the robot went down it. I think we should reserve judgment on whether or not it's our 'friend.'"

"Worrier," Dex teased, but Santiago replied with complete seriousness.

"I can afford to lose the repair bot, Dex. I cannot afford to lose you."

Dex crept to the corridor, peeking around the edge and finding it empty before moving ahead. Despite the vacuum of space, he imagined his footsteps clanging against the bulkhead, sending out a signal to any guards around engineering. Surely the crew had automated bots for that purpose. Yet they had no way to keep an enemy from cutting holes in their hull. "We cannot afford to lose this ship, Santiago. Our fates are tied together now. We'll either help each other live or destroy each other. Any one-sided victory here will mean death for us both."

"And you know this, *how?*"

"Call it a hunch. At the very least, we need parts for that shield generator, and if this bot fails, that leaves me to do the scavenging."

He made his stealthy way along the empty corridors, pausing at junctions, checking above as well as to the sides, following Santiago's cues as he recounted the route of their shanghaied robot. Now and again, a robot on its way to some unknown task would pass by, but if Dex stood still against the wall, it ignored him. At first, nervousness and adrenaline coursed through his veins and heightened his senses, but after minutes of empty nothingness, that same adrenaline made him edgy.

"How long does this go on?" he growled.

"Another right in about thirty meters, and you will enter the hall leading to the main chamber. Are you all right?"

No, I am not all right. This ship is not all right. Scarlet is not all right—

Dex stopped and clenched his fists against memories that threatened to over-take him. *Focus*, he told himself as he felt the tingle of the medical bracelet.

Beautiful Scarlet, vibrant Scarlet, losing her luster as the disease ate away at her.

"Dammit, not now!" he hissed. It was ri-diculous. When he'd gotten the diagnosis of Disk Activated Memory Disorder, he'd re-moved all signs of her from his ship, trusting Santiago to care for the images and logs, locking away the few mementos he could not bear to part with, even banishing her fa-vorite foods. For years, he'd suffered the loneliness rather than have anything that would trigger an unwanted walk down Memory Lane, when a stroll might cost him his life or the ship. He'd forced his mind to other things, endured losing her in his thoughts as well as his presence. Yet, here on a stupid empty ship, alien from anything they'd ever shared, she threatened to take over his mind?

How his arms ached with the memory of holding her!

"Dex?" Santiago's voice was a distant whisper.

Think about something else, Dex.

"Dex, are you all right?"

"Where are all the bodies?" Dex managed to blurt out, channeling his anger into a mystery that had nagged at the corners of his mind. He pulled it to the forefront, fueled it, let it overwhelm the image of his wife and the loneliness that threatened to leave him curled up in a corner of an alien ship. "I've been moving deeper and deeper into this ship for over ten minutes, and I still haven't seen a single body—nothing organic, for that matter. So where are they?"

"The repair bot has not seen any bodies, either. Perhaps the crew abandoned ship?"

The conversation helped. Dex again pushed himself off the wall and continued down the hall. "Hard to believe. It's still functioning, and we didn't see that much damage. Scan the hull; do you see anything that might indicate escape pods?"

"Does it matter?"

"Humor me."

A pause, then, "The schematics don't show anything resembling escape pods. The next left, please."

He checked the turn, then took it. "You have schematics for the entire ship? Check for living quarters, kitchen facilities. Bathrooms."

He froze as a repair bot scurried above him, its legs poking in and out of the holes. He was struck with its grace. For a moment, he had an image of his mother's cross stitch, how the needle darted in and out of the fabric with smooth efficiency. Did these people have arts they did at their leisure? Did they believe in leisure?

They had myths, but it's not the same. No, the Elomijans have myths; we don't know anything about these people. "Well?"

"I find nothing," Santiago replied. "Go carefully. See the opening at your right? That's the main chamber. Our robot has stopped there."

"No doors, either? I've not seen a single vaccing door. What kind of people don't want a little privacy? Or are the doors retracted into the walls?" He paused at the doorless entrance, curling a finger around the threshold. With whispered commands, he directed the radar to operate from his glove and project the view onto his screen. One of his apprentices—Xan Whitestar, wasn't it? Not Kixek... Yes, Xan, always tinkering; drove him nuts, but Scarlet encouraged it... Xan had loved toying with the spacesuits. He'd thought the feature foolish at the time; now, he thanked Xan Whitestar, and Scarlet for insisting that Dex "indulge the boy."

The room was easily half the size of the *Santiago*. The strobing, monochrome images on his faceplate showed swarms of smaller repair bots crawling over machinery attached at all angles on the spherical surface of the engine room. Most of the machines remained a mystery to him, though he could guess at weapons systems, propulsion, navigation—and the shield generator they so desperately needed. He spotted a larger repair bot, crumpled in the corner. His heart spasmed. "Santiago, where's our bot?"

"Two o'clock and thirty degrees ascension."

He sighed with relief and directed his attention to the right and up. Their bot was pulling something off a shield generator. He had the sudden urge to rush in himself, rip the generator out entirely, and return to his ship to cannibalize it there.

A smaller bot approached the repair bot. He waited with held breath as it hovered and his bot continued on its mission. Were they talking? Did it suspect?

"Santiago, get out of its brain."

"Not yet, I—"

The smaller bot backed away and fired its laser. The repair bot jerked as the thin beam pierced through its central processors. It lost its grip and floated away, pulling a rod and an oddly shaped cylinder with it. Dex recognized the parts as the ones burned out on the *Santiago's* CivB shield generator.

The smaller bot glided toward the robot, extending small arms.

"Oh, no, you don't!" Without pausing to consider his actions, Dex released the magnets in his boots, pushed himself off the floor and flew toward the pieces, hands outstretched.

"Dex! I lost the robot," Santiago called out.

"Lock down your systems!" Even though he had farther to move, his speed let him get to the damaged bot before its attacker. He grabbed the parts as he swung the bot around, smashing it into the oncoming bot. Knocked off-kilter, its shot went wild, searing a hole in a generator.

A silent fury of activity let loose.

Dozens of repair bots swarmed to the damaged system while some launched themselves at the attacking bot, tearing it apart. In the moment of distraction, he yanked hard at the parts he needed, pulling them from the grip of the repair bot. Dex hit the back wall with his feet and launched himself out the door.

Halfway to the door, several robots spun to face him. Three knitted their way across the ceiling, moving fast. One blocked his way. He lifted the rod he'd snatched from the repair bot and swung. Metal cracked against metal. The robot fell.

"Careful! We need that," Santiago warned.

"Nag, nag. I'm busy!" He saw the first turn coming, and threw his body to the right, barely catching the wall with an outstretched arm. His bicep smacked the corner; his shoulder wrenched, but he pushed off anyway and soared through the long, empty corridor.

"That was easy enough," he muttered.

"Or not. Behind you!"

Dex switched his view to the rear. A swarm of thirty or more of the spidery bots was rounding the corner and skittering his way.

"Dex, twist right!"

He jerked, losing momentum, as a beam of light and heat passed where he'd been. "Vac!"

"Next left corridor," Santiago said.

"That's the wrong way." He dove and spun, keeping himself a moving target. Another laser passed overhead.

"Trust me. Now!"

With a howl that was half-protest/half-effort, Dex jackknifed his body and pushed into the smaller corridor. His helmet bumped something, and the rod he carried snagged.

"Are you nuts? It's a maze in here! They'll catch me."

"Not if you move quickly, and all the machinery will make it difficult and dangerous to shoot."

"Hope you're right." He ordered his boots to one-eighth magnetic force and used his feet to push him while he scrambled to secure on his suit the spare parts he'd liberated. With his hands free, he moved faster, but not fast enough. It was like climbing Squatty Mountain, only he was out of practice and out of shape, and the ridge had narrowed so that he bumped against out-croppings of rock.

No, Dex, machinery. Machinery in the alien ship. Focus!

His breath sounded loud to his own ears, and sweat trickled down his forehead. He blinked but didn't dare shake his head for fear of splattering his faceplate with sweat. The split view showed the maze of equipment ahead, and the robots gaining behind.

"I'm losing my lead. Find me a clear corridor."

"Three meters, then up and to the right. Take it to the fork, then right. Move fast."

"I'm getting winded. Check the blueprints. I need a hidey-hole. I'll let them pass ahead of me, then double back."

"Keep moving. There are no hidey-holes on this ship."

"If I break something here, will they try to fix it?"

"Unknown."

"Don't sound like that backup computer you keep complaining about," Dex scolded. He planted his boot on the next outcropping and pushed up, twisted to avoid a mechanical widget that took half the space in front of him and forced the so-called clear path to curl to the left and back, and grabbed at the edge of a junction.

He reached the corridor, braced himself against the wall, and shoved hard with his legs. Sharp pain lanced through his right leg as he sailed down the corridor. "Dammit, there are always hidey-holes. Find one."

"Not on this ship."

Nothing moved behind him—yet—but the sharp V of the fork was coming at him at far too fast. He twisted right. "What kind of stupid ship doesn't have a place to hide?"

"A ship not built for people!"

Dex threw his arm up to protect his helmet as he crashed into the right side of the fork, missing the edge of the V. Ignoring the pain of impact, he pushed off again. His radar caught several of the bots entering the long hall. "A drone, this large? Dammit! Where next?"

Another long corridor he managed without incident, then a second claustrophobic tangle of pipes and levers that Santiago insisted was a short cut.

Dex laughed at the small exit that stood between him and the last corridor to his ship and freedom. "I can't squeeze through that!"

"I've done the measurements. You have inches to spare."

"Including the spare parts I'm lugging for you? What about that corridor I passed earlier?"

"Dead end, unless you *want* to go back toward the army of bots chasing you."

"Great." He checked behind. No bots storming after him just yet, but there was too much equipment in this narrow confine; they could be only steps behind him. "Santiago?"

"Can you put them out first?"

Dex swore. The equipment around him already brushed his shoulders and snagged against the life support equipment on his back. He'd have to back up to a clearer spot and risk capture if he wanted to maneuver the spare parts ahead of him.

"Leave them behind," Santiago urged. "We'll find another way—maybe send a repair bot after them."

"Vac that! I'm not risking my own equipment. Have that airlock open and ready." He reached down, grasped the rod. It was narrow enough to push ahead. The oddly shaped cylinder would never get past his chest, but he'd seen its burned-out brother in the *Santiago's* shield generator. He didn't even know what it did, but he knew they needed this part if they wanted their shields back to full function. With difficulty, he arched up, pressing his back against the equipment above him. He grabbed the over-sized part, feeling around for the release catch on his belt. He fumbled at the clip, freed the part, and pushed it down as he pulled himself forward. He caught it between his boots.

The effort left him shaking, but he didn't dare pause. The airlock lay just past the exit hole.

Risking losing his view from behind, he repeated his earlier trick of sliding his gloved hand around the exit and looking at the large corridor beyond. Nothing to the interior.

A second horde of bots crawled around the edge of the damaged hull.

"Vac!" He drew his hand in quickly. No way to avoid them, and he had to get out of the ship. *So, push off fast and hard. Use the other wall to ricochet straight out the hole and to the* Santiago. He took three deep, strong breaths, steeling himself, then gripped the edges of the porthole and pulled himself through.

His backpack caught on the wall. With a howl of protest over his lost momentum, he backed up, pushed his stomach flat against the lower edge of the opening and tried again. As soon as he came free, he twisted into a somersault and grabbed the spare part from his booted grip. He magnetized the boots and ran.

He'd taken three steps when his rear view showed the spider bots spewing from the exit hole he'd just squeezed out of.

Ignoring his leg's protests, he put on more speed as he drew his relic gun and set it for the widest beam.

The bots around the gaping hole in the hull jerked with the sudden pulse of energy. He didn't think he'd shut them down, but there was no time to shoot them all again.

He launched himself.

He flew through the hole before the bots around it could react and sailed into the safety of the *Santiago's* airlock. Two or three lasers scored on the interior of the ship before Santiago could shut the doors.

Dex lay on the floor, catching his breath and enjoying the pull of artificial gravity. When he could again breathe without gasping, he lifted his head and saw the blackened metal where a laser had missed him by mere inches. He'd come so close to dying.

And yet, I feel more alive than I have in ages. He laughed.

"I fail to find anything funny in our situation," Santiago said.

"Scarlet never did either, friend. Scarlet never did, either."

Chapter Eight

"*Space deceives; it holds no emptiness/rather its dangers lie hidden/too impersonal for even an ambush.*"

Scarlet's voice pulled Dex's attention from the powdered eggs he'd been pushing around with his fork. "What?"

"*Space deceives; it holds no emptiness/rather its dangers lie hidden/too impersonal for even an ambush.* So, is that creepy or exciting?"

"Literary. What are you reading?"

"'Planetside Dreams.' You won't like it—no schematics or equations." Although her tone was teasing, her focus remained on the pad beside her half-eaten breakfast.

"Since when did you start liking that leak?" When she shrugged, he asked, "Are you homesick?"

"For a planet?" His space-born wife raised a brow at him. He loved when she did that; it never failed to send a thrill along his spine. Today, however, he looked around the cramped quarters of their ship, at the pre-packaged food rehydrated with water recycled from their own sweat and urine, at the window where deceptive space waited with its impersonal dangers that would leave you just as dead as any ambush, and he asked again, "Do you want to go home?"

"This is home, Dex. What a silly question."

He threw down his fork and slouched in his chair. "Then why are you reading that fuzz-brained static?"

"Answer my question, and you just might answer yours." She returned to her book, leaving him to grumble over his cold eggs.

The scene dissolved. Scarlet blurred and brightened while everything else darkened to reds and blacks. Then, Dex stood on the Bloody Road, the deceptive emptiness of space around him, the glowing brilliance of the goddess before.

"An interesting woman," Elomij commented.

"Frustrating woman," Dex corrected, his mind and heart still on the memory.

The goddess' laughter flowed over him like sunshine: warm, comforting, yet impersonal. Did she hold secret dangers as well?

"Your Scarlet knew you too well. She played both predator and prey for you, Hunter, crafting new mysteries to confound you."

Dex snorted. "Oh, she was good at that."

"It kept you interested. And you loved her for it." The goddess sighed, then, and her gaze moved from Dex to through him and down the pathway.

Dex glanced behind him but did not see her consort.

"Hudon doesn't deserve you."

She laughed, surprised. "Bold talk from a mortal."

"Wisdom from someone outside your time. I'd like to think I interested Scarlet as much as she interested me. That's what marriage should be."

Her eyes flashed. "You presume too much, mortal! You have passed your second test, though Hudon is not impressed by your scurrying like a rodent. Nonetheless, I give you this prize. The greatest danger is to come; and impersonal, it is not. You will lose all to win."

"A riddle? That's it? I don't remember ever asking to be part of this contest."

Elomij raised her brow in a perfect imitation of Scarlet. "You never did."

Dex snapped back to the present to find himself sitting at the table, powdered eggs before him, smothered in the dawlsu Molly had sent. On the viewscreen, the captured ship surged ahead. Although a blur to his unaided eyesight, Dex could see it was still tied to the grapplers and bore the wound he had inflicted on it. Some of the bots he'd hit with the relic gun on his way out had apparently been damaged as well, and they floated in the safe emptiness between the ship and the *Santiago*.

He squinted his eyes shut, dispelling the fading images of Scarlet and Elomij, then looked at his medical bracelet. It showed hours since it last activated.

Just dozed, then. He felt a small relief at that. He'd earned a few minutes' rest. Nonetheless, he'd done enough woolgathering. "Santiago, how're those parts holding up?"

"Your repairs have increased shield efficiency by 42 percent. We are nearly on par with our prey's protective ability."

"With just the CivB?" His hopes rose.

"No. That is counting my inherent shielding as well."

"Figures." He chuckled and stabbed at his eggs with his fork. "It might be that our wounded friend will have to bring us across the void and back to reality instead of vice-versa."

"I am not prepared to call it 'friend.' It tried to kill you. It got us into this mess in the first place."

Dex shrugged. "It's just doing its job. When we get back, I'm not just selling it to the highest bidder. No, that ship deserves respect. How's your computing ability? Better?"

"I am able to take on further tasks."

Dex took a large gulp of coffee. "Scan our contacts. Find a couple that will treat this ship like the find it is."

"Dex," Santiago took on a mildly scolding tone. It reminded him of Scarlet. "Don't you think that's premature considering our plight?"

As if to affirm his assertion, the proximity alarms started howling.

"Civilization A attack drone on intercept course," the backup computer intoned.

"What? Show me! Santiago, evasive!" Dex slammed down the last of his coffee and shoved his half-empty plate into a drawer where it would not be cast about should the inertial dampeners fail.

"I can't," Santiago replied, "unless you wish me to disengage from our prey. The best I can do is try to put the ship between us and that drone, which our prey is not keen on our doing, I should add. Shall I disengage grapplers?"

Dex swore. "We are not losing that ship. Fine. We fight. Withdraw one capture beam and prepare to energize it. Ready the cutting laser. Might as well take a trick from our friend's repair bots."

"It will have to get in close. I cannot guarantee accuracy at this distance."

Dex watched the screen as the drone sped toward them, a larger red circle around it showing the estimated weapon's distance based on others of its kind. Or rather, based on what researchers thought their accurate shooting distance was. For once, he hoped they'd overestimated. A green circle emanating from Santiago marked the best distance for their own laser. Despite their laser being industrial and not weapons grade, they had a slight advantage.

"Is it heading for us or our prey?"

"Our prey. It's slowing. I think it's not sure what to do about us."

Slowing was good, but if it stopped before it got into the *Santiago's* laser range, they'd be sitting ducks. "What's our prey doing?"

"Nothing."

"What?" He stepped toward the viewscreen, pulling on the spectacles. The captured ship continued to surge ahead, but otherwise made no move to evade or fight. Had it given up? Or had it recognized them as its master, and thus as its protector?

Either way, if that drone changed course to the front of their captured ship, it would be out of the *Santiago's* range while able to inflict its own damage. In that case, neither their prey nor they stood a chance. They had to draw that drone in.

"Let's move. Release only what grapplers you need in order to roll to the side. Show them the ship's wounded."

"Dex?"

"Bait, Santiago. Let that drone see the ship's weak spot. It will maneuver to get a good shot...and then we take it out."

"And if our prey bolts?"

Dex shook his head. "It won't. We have a common foe."

"Retracting grapplers. Capture beam two disengaged. Rolling..."

Through the soles of his feet, Dex felt the *Santiago* tilt as it followed the curve of their ship. On the screen, the *Santiago's* icon twisted along the hull of their prey, revealing a white dot marking the hole Dex had cut. He muttered encouragement as he watched the drone alter course.

Suddenly the ship lurched around him.

"Dex, it's bolting!"

"I can see that!" On the screen, the distance between the captured ship and the *Santiago* stretched. "Hang on! Is our drone pursuing?"

"Yes, faster now. I think it wants to get a good shot."

"We're not giving it that chance. Fire lasers and zap it with that capture beam as soon as they are in ra—" He cut off his words when the viewscreen showed Santiago doing just that.

"No need to tell me twice," the AI replied.

Again, the *Santiago* lurched, nearly throwing Dex. He saw a beam of light from the drone just miss the ship, as the kitchen window flared amber.

"Evading. Zapping it again. Dex, sit down and strap in. I don't want you breaking more bones." The floor slid under Dex as if to emphasize the point.

With a howl of frustration, Dex threw himself into a kitchen chair and pulled at the straps he'd almost forgotten about. They were meant for passengers, not the pilot of his own ship! He watched, helpless, as Santiago fought with the drone of one species while being pulled by the ship of another. The deck heaved under his feet as the energy bursts played on the shields. His grip tightened on the arm of the chair, making the plastic creak. He should be helping!

He watched pulses move from the *Santiago* to the drone as his friend tried to blast out its systems by sending shocks through the capture beam. The drone fired back. Dex winced as Santiago's shields lit up with blinding flashes, but the drone's shots were all glancing blows. Maybe Santiago had at least confused its targeting systems. Meanwhile, the map on the viewscreen changed as their prey brought them closer to a swarl.

A swarl!

"*Santi*—" A blast threw him forward against the restraints. Behind him, he heard the whine and popping of electronics on overload. Smoke once more trickled in from the hall.

"One more like that, and we'll lose the shield."

"Then don't get hit! Is the ship resisting the beam?"

"Yes, but not successfully."

"See that swarl? When we get close, let it go."

"Release the drone?"

A flash of light, this time an angry red. They were getting close.

"Yes! Push it if you can. Knock it into the swarl!"

Santiago didn't reply, but Dex saw the beam on the viewscreen change. Concave waves pounded the drone, then stopped abruptly as they neared the upturning of the matter stream. They and their prey sped by as the drone got caught in the swirling mass and was flung away from them.

"Ha!" Dex slapped his chair and tried to stand, the restraints pulling him back down. "That's how we do it. Good work, my friend. Now return to our previous position and get those grapplers on. We don't want our prey to think it's going to get rid of us now, right, Santiago?"

Silence.

"Santiago!"

The backup computer answered. "Fire in engineering. AI in protective mode."

"Vac!" Dex pulled the release catch of the restraints and flew out of his chair, ignoring the protests of his own body. On the way, he yanked off his glasses, tossing them aside, his mind only on how they'd interfere with the firefighting mask he'd need. He thundered to engineering. He shoved at the partially closed door, slid down the ladder, and dashed in, pausing to grab the fire gear—a mask and oxygen converter and the extinguisher.

He took only enough time to assess the situation without letting himself react emotionally. Pockets of flames ate at the systems and the ship's air. Normally, the ship would have sealed the doors and vented the air from the room, but the structural damage prevented it. The room was a blurry, smoked-filled maze, but he didn't need clear vision to make out the flames. He pointed the extinguisher at the fire, concentrating on short, controlled blasts. One section calmed to smoldering, and he moved on. Not much should have burned in this room, but years of neglect had left the dirt and oils the flames needed.

"I'm sorry. I'm sorry," Dex repeated with each burst from his extinguisher. "I'm so sorry, old friend."

He fired at the last of the flames, then again at some smoldering areas threatening to revive. Satisfied, he dropped the extinguisher and leaned against one of the consoles. He paused, panting, then pulled off the mask to conserve the oxygen in its tanks. Who knew when he might need it again? "Santiago. Please respond. *Santiago*? Computer, status of the AI."

"Assessing."

"Well, while you're assessing, move us back to our original position, re-engage the capture beam, and deploy the grapplers. I don't want our prey thinking it's going to lose us."

"Complying."

While the computer enacted his commands and did its triage, Dex dragged the fire gear back to its place, doing a quick clean-up and check to make sure it was ready for the next emergency. The smoke ticked his throat and lungs, triggering painful coughs.

"That ship will be the death of me," he muttered as he ascended the ladder, yet he knew that it had become the life of him as well. Fair trade off.

He found his glasses lodged in a half-open panel. He reached for them, but instinct made him draw back and circle in for a closer look. One earpiece sat among a tangle of wires that were half-pulled from their connections and bare in spots.

He groaned.

He ordered the computer to cut power to the area, but nonetheless retrieved some heavy gloves from the kitchen to grab the glasses. With everything else that had gone wrong, he wasn't going to risk getting electrocuted by his own ship. Fortunately, the glasses looked undamaged; sturdy stuff, those nanites. Next, he spent another ten minutes securing the wires and panel. Fortunately, that panel handled power to the bedroom. As he worked, the computer gave updates on the repair of the *Santiago*. The AI, it reported in its disinterested tone, was in a regenerative coma. The last strike from the drone had overpowered its systems.

Which means it got past the shields. Dex shivered at how close they'd come. "Status of the CivB shield generator?"

"Civilization B Generator was offline for 320 microseconds and is now operating at 75 percent capacity."

Dex released the breath he was holding. "When will Santiago come out of his coma?"

"No less than seven hours."

Dex sat back on his heels and rested his head in his hands. He was tired. If they got out of this—no, *once* they got out of this— he was going to sleep for weeks. A coma would suit him just fine, and Santiago could stay awake, handle repairs, and worry.

But for now, he was not going to stand by helpless while his ship fought their battles. If his ship recovered well enough to fight their battles again. He needed a nav console, and he needed an interface.

He pushed himself to his feet, then paused as the complaints of his body made themselves known before subsiding. The ship, he thought with a pang of guilt, looked worse than he felt: Smoke coated the air in a light haze, and at least one fracture in the wall had grown large enough for him to put a hand through. The damage he'd just fixed was probably some of the most minor of their concerns. He could have left it, hidden it behind the re-attached panel for someday when he had time.

Someday. How many things have I left waiting for someday? I never used to be like that. I used to keep this ship in top condition. I let it get ahead of me. No desire to go to a station for refit, no apprentices to help, no Scarlet...

"I'm sorry, Scarlet. Maybe it's just as well you aren't here to see what's become of the pride of your family's business." He rubbed the wall affectionately, apologizing to it, too, and in his mind's eye, he saw his father-in-law caressing the bulkhead to the kitchen, his eyes gleaming with pride and affection.

Dex and Scarlet had made the long trip from Keldar Station, a trip fraught with delays and annoyances that had left them snappy and exhausted. All that was forgotten when they arrived, and they'd only paused long enough to drop their small bags at her parents' apartment before hurrying to the family shipyard to see their ship. They started by gazing out the viewport. Scarlet, ever the shipbuilder's daughter, explained to him that the shell was an old *Lewis*-class, retired from the Antares Starforces, but still one of the strongest and most able designs in the fleet—or just about any fleet, for that matter. "They were scout ships, built for speed and maneuverability in and out of atmosphere, so they had to handle the G-stress."

"Quite right, daughter," Permillion Dane surprised them with his presence. He accepted her hug with the dignity of a man more comfortable around machines than people, then continued. "Now, everyone's depending on improved shielding to take the strain, but when the *Lewises* were built, they valued hull strength. Forty-point-two meters bow to stern, seventeen in diameter at its thickest. Two airlocks. We expanded one to industrial size and tore out most of the rooms around it to make small and large storage for your finds. Second airlock is more standard; figured you'd use it for docking so no one's tempted by your treasures."

Scarlet chuckled. "You left escape pods?"

"Of course." He touched a pad on the window, and a schematic of the ship replaced the view. He pointed at two points up and stern, and down and aft. "That last is by the bridge. She's a beauty; built for six, but we replaced everything with controls for two—one, if you employ the AI. Five hundred square feet living space—that's three cabins, kitchen and dining, and a small meeting room. Most of your space is going to storage, your engines, of course, and that shield generator."

Her father shook his head. "Never seen anything like it. We did our best with the information you gave us, but you're going to want to work with it and put it through some trials before I release the ship to you. So, that, and of course, your AI. I have never heard your cousin Gilly swear so much in his career, Scarlet."

Scarlet gave Dex's arm a happy squeeze, and he returned her smile. She'd told him about Gilly's reputation for profanity, and how one could almost plot it to predict the success of a project. The last time the programmer had seared the paint off the walls with his curses was when programming the AI they used at Keldar to map the Disk.

"Can we see it? Can we talk to it now?" Scarlet asked, her eyes alight with excitement.

Her father gave her an affectionate smile. "Tomorrow. Gilly's just about got his voice back, so he's ready for whatever tweaking you need done."

They did a walk-through of the ship with her father and an assistant to write down any flaws or modifications needed. Permillion and his people had outdone themselves, and they knew it, but he never released a ship without the approval of his customers.

They returned to the kitchen, where her father had caressed one bracing column as though it were the arm of a child and regarded them both with a pleased but expectant smile. "Well?"

Scarlet answered by throwing her arms around him and squealing. "It's perfect, Daddy!"

"Have to admit, I'm impressed." Dex held out his hand.

Permillion took it. "Nothing but the best for my little girl, and my amazing son-in-law."

Dex laughed, derisively. "I'm not amazing, sir."

Permillion raised a brow as Scarlet huffed. "Right. And who not only captured a CivB ship with a working anti-spaghettification shield but figured out how to adapt it to our technology?"

He twitched his shoulders at his father-in-law. "Your people did that."

His father-in-law released his hand. "With your direction—and you still need to modify it. And you did retrieve the generator intact."

"And alone." Scarlet's tone was scolding rather than proud. "I'd never been so worried in my life. Stuck in the control center at Keldar, helpless to do anything."

"Excuse me? You were my navigator."

"By proxy! And once you got into the time dilation, not even then." She stepped away from her father, her eyes flashing, fists clenched as if she could strangle the memories of her fear. "Hours, and then days of waiting to know if anything I said helped—if you were even alive. And when you hit that swarl, and we didn't hear from you for a month... I went to bed each night thinking..."

She swallowed hard. Her eyes filled with tears, but she snapped, "Never again, Dex Hollister. You will never put me through that again!"

Her father looked at his feet, embarrassed at his daughter's passionate display.

Dex pulled her into an embrace. "Never again. We're a team now—you and me."

"And your AI," Permillion interjected, relieved to bring the subject back to ships and engineering and away from the uncomfortable messiness of his daughter's emotions. "We'll install it after you've had a chance to meet it in the lab and approve it. Now, as for the name of your ship...?"

Dex was about to say, "Intrepid," but Scarlet spoke first. "Santiago!"

Dex eyed his wife quizzically, but her father buckled over laughing. For all his discomfort with serious emotions, he was always ready to react to something he found funny.

"This an old boyfriend?" Dex asked, suspicion edging his voice.

"Worse—a vid star!" her father supplied between chortles. "Much harder to compete with."

Dex's brows knit together. His family, out on the frontier and busy with the wildlife preserve, never had virtual reality videos. He'd only discovered them when coming stationside, and some had been very...intense...experiences. Scarlet had brought a vidset to Keldar, a present from her sister, but he didn't remember any vids starring a Santiago.

"There's no competition!" Scarlet protested, which only made her father laugh louder.

She wrapped her arms around her husband and tilted her chin to gaze straight into his eyes. "There's no competition."

"Don't worry," her father straightened, wiping his cheeks. He often shied away from tears of anger or sadness, but never those resulting from a good laugh. "We never let her or her sister get anything past the 'light romance' rating. So, Dex—Santiago?"

He studied Scarlet's glowing face. They'd be having a longer conversation about this "Santiago" later, and whether she or her sister had enjoyed some of his other vids without Daddy's knowledge.

Her smile turned knowing, and her hands slid down his back. "You *know* there's no competition," she purred.

Thus, the challenge was given. "Santiago, it is."

The memory faded with a tingle of the medical bracelet, but Dex continued to feel disoriented. What had happened to his ship? Where were Scarlet and Permillion? He stared at his gloved hands, holding the spectacles, trying to control his breathing as his mind fought its way to the present.

When it did, however, it arrived with a flash of insight, and he hurried to the small storage room to grab the hydraulic spanner. Dragging the heavy machine back to the bedroom door, he inserted it into the gap near the bottom and turned it on, supporting it as the jaws opened, pushing the door away from the threshold. Metal bent with groans of protest heard even above the growling of the spanner's engine. When the gap looked large enough to get his legs through, he clicked it off and repositioned it. His arms protested the weight, but the gap here was already wider, and it took less time. When it looked wide enough, he pulled out the spanner and let it fall with a clunk. He shook out his arms while he caught his breath, coughing when his lungs' demand for oxygen made him inhale too deeply.

He slid through the opening to the bedroom, and, ignoring the mess around him and the brilliant kaleidoscope of colors in the window that marked distant swarls, he threw open a cabinet door. Objects, broken and pulled from their containers by the transition into the black hole, fell on and around him, but he was only interested in one.

"Come on, come on..." He dug through the mess, then reached to the back of the top shelf. "Yes!"

He pulled down the silver case and opened it. Nestled in sturdy packaging were the gloves and interface of Scarlet's VR gear and its console. Long gloves with external wires to translate movements into the vid and give tactile sensations in return. The skullcap, also covered in wires and sensors, transmitted the sounds and sent sensations along the spine. The goggles provided full holographic vision, to a clearer degree than the holograms he used, and could be adjusted to different focus levels. Tactile sensations would be mostly virtual, but better than what he had now, which was nothing. He'd lose some reaction time, and he'd have to trust Santiago to finesse his movements, but at least he wouldn't be left sitting aside like some spectator in his own fight. The set looked nearly new. She hadn't used it often, and they'd never bought a set for him. He never liked artificial pleasures.

"Thank you, Scarlet!" He clutched the case in a tight grip and slid back out and to the bridge, calling for one of his repair bots. It would be a patch job, but if he were lucky, he would be able to adapt the console and gear to allow him to interface with Santiago and the nav system.

He gave a sad laugh when he saw the torn console. Torn console, torn walls, bent doors... He'd have to replace the entire ship when they got back.

No matter; as long as I still have Santiago and the shields...and our prize. "I didn't let you go before, and I won't let you go now. We'll emerge from this pit together, or we'll die together trying. You hear me?" Anger and determination filled him anew, and his voice rose until he was shouting. "Do you hear me?"

"Please restate the question," the computer replied.

He heaved a sigh, deflating. "Never mind. No, wait. Any more legends in that file Molly sent us?" He had hours of tedious work ahead of him; might as well have some entertainment.

"There are twenty-two legends, with commentary."

"Skip the commentary. Let's hear some more about Elomij and the Bloody Road."

"*Elomij and Hudon Create the Bloody Road.*"

At first, there were the People, brothers all, yet split. And thus split, they lived in ignorance of each other. That ignorance was nurtured by Welga, goddess of bliss, and with the ignorance came peace and joy. And Welga was happy, and the People likewise.

But Elomij, goddess of beauty and change, watched the People under Welga's bliss, and saw stagnation, and in that stagnation, the Gentle Sleep. She yearned for the People to awaken.

So she fashioned for the People a jeweled eye of great beauty. Within that jeweled eye, she placed the desire to see beyond the present, so that the People would move past their contentment into growth. Then Elomij dressed in her finest raiment and journeyed to the Eternal Fields. There, she met her friend Welga, and begged permission to give the People a gift. But Welga saw the desires hidden in the eye and turned her back on Elomij.

Elomij fled the Fields, watering them with her tears. Where her tears fell, bits of eternity clung to them and they caught fire. Those tears became the stars that fill the night sky, and it is said that Elomij's grief will someday overpower the eternity in each, and one by one, the stars will fade and die.

Hudon, god of war, had seen Welga spurn Elomij. Long had he wanted the goddess of beauty. The other gods had ostracized the god of war and the violence he brought with him, but with Elomij at his side, he would again have a place of honor among them. He approached Welga and with sweet words and deceit, learned of Elomij's gift. So he hatched a plan that would not only win him the fair goddess, but further his trade as well.

He went to Elomij and seduced her with talk of innovation and evolution. He listened to her desires for the People and shared in them. Together, they made a new plan to deliver Elomij's gift.

Again, Elomij approached Welga, but this time, she begged Welga to show her the People in their contentment, so that she might learn such peace herself. And as Welga and Elomij walked along the Golden Road of Now, Hudon took the jeweled eye to the people. However, before he delivered Elomij's gift, he carried it to the lands of Despair, a wilderness of darkness and desiccation. There, he surveyed the stones before him, searching for the perfect shard to add to the eye. Fear was too sickly and cast a pall over the other jewels. Distrust was too pale; hate too harsh. He wandered further and found the perfect stone. Conflict, with its myriad faces, complemented the many beauties of the eye and would stay hidden among its glamour until the perfect time.

He removed one tiny jewel and replaced it with one of conflict. He threw Elomij's jewel aside, and where it fell, a small, beautiful flower grew. That flower became known as Hope, and it always grows within despair, but one must look closely to find it. Once found *and nurtured, however, it can blossom into a large bush, and its perfume overpowers the stench of despair and heals the soul.*

Then he hid the Eye where the people would find it. He courted Elomij as they waited its discovery.

When the People at last came upon the Eye of Elomij, they found it pleasing. For a time, it merely amused them, so that Welga did not realize the gift she had forbidden had been given and accepted. But with time and use, the People began to see more, to want more. Their bliss weakened, and with it, Welga.

Elomij watched with interest and pride the growth of the People. For the People were no longer just intelligent animals. They sought learning and advancement. They moved beyond their homes, beyond even the secure embrace of their own worlds. Hudon praised Elomij for her victory, and her attachment to him grew.

Then, the People, once separate and content, met, and the jewel of conflict, having found its perfect time, blazed over the eye, clouding their vision. With conflict came competition and violence. Yet Elomij's power was strong, and the jewels of the Eye still vi-

brant. Thus did conflict also excite courage, honor, patriotism, and glory.

Nonetheless, bliss was no more, and Welga waned in the People's darkness. Elomij, saddened and guilt-ridden, cared for her friend, but even her careful ministrations could not revive her. Hudon stood by, playing the faithful consort of Elomij, and the goddesses did not see the greedy gleam in his eye.

Elomij repented of her gift for her friend's sake, yet the goddess of change was excited by the advances of the People, and Hudon fueled that fire even as the People created their own fire to lash out against each other. And the Golden Road became stained with their blood.

Chapter Nine

Santiago came back online as Dex was putting his new interface through its paces.

"About time," he growled at the AI's greeting. "How are you?"

"Sluggish," Santiago replied. "And confused. Not so much that you would notice, perhaps, but enough to make me uncomfortable."

"Well, find a way to get comfortable. We've got work ahead of us."

If the machine in Santiago wanted to note its damage and the effects, at least the intelligence in Santiago knew better than to bother. "I see that you've been busy. You installed the docking tube to our captured ship."

"Our fates are tied together. It recognizes that."

"And when it decides our fates are no longer linked?"

"It won't, not now. We need each other. We win together or die together."

A pause, then, "As I said, I am sluggish and confused."

Dex chuckled. "No, my friend, you just haven't correlated the right data." With a quick series of hand commands, he called up the sensor data from seven and a half hours ago. "I didn't like that that drone came on us so unexpectedly, so I back-traced its path."

Despite Santiago's claims, he didn't hesitate to voice his conclusion. "It came from further toward the singularity."

"Exactly."

"I didn't have sensors focused there. We weren't near any swarls or hyperaccelerated activity. There shouldn't have been any way a drone could have come up from there."

"And yet, somehow, it did."

"I'm readjusting sensors."

"Already done while you were sleeping," Dex interrupted. "Keep up with me."

As he'd expected, the AI took his challenge and moved ahead. "If that drone came from deeper in the singularity, then it has equipment to warp the gravity field—which means it can escape the swarl. Did it return?"

Dex let out a grunt of surprise. That was an angle he hadn't considered. "You must have knocked out some of its systems after all. However, if a simple drone can escape the singularity..."

"...then perhaps our prey can, as well? And if it can, then it will escape—but not with its hull compromised. Thus, the docking tube—and I see our human-made shield has been expanded to cover the area. We are interdependent."

"For the duration, at any rate. I need you to go over those schematics you got from that repair bot."

"Already processing. We can assume that the system is offline, as the ship did not attempt to re-cross the event horizon."

"Or it felt more comfortable in its own territory. It knew about those swarls, both the one it tried to lose us with and the one we used to scrape off that drone. No, look at this telemetry from the drone." He singled out a small anomalous blip the backup computer had found in the sea of confusion. Hope argued that it was just that—an anomaly, probably the result of overstressed systems—but Dex wasn't the hopeful type.

Thus, neither was Santiago. "A signal—back into the singularity. Which means there will be more coming. Dex, the probability of our surviving a coordinated attack from a multitude of drones is slim."

"We're experts in slim chances. For that matter, I'm wondering how we managed to survive this attack. Consider: all the drones we've ever dealt with in the Disk have been damaged, drives nonfunctional, weapons systems shot; the only thing active were their shields. We just went up against a fully functioning war drone."

"Not fully," Santiago amended. "One side was damaged. I focused the capture beam there to keep that side facing us. It minimized the number of lasers in our direction."

"Smart move, that, but it still shot at us and missed for the most part."

"It hit often enough to knock me offline."

"Not saying we came out of it unscathed, but it should have been able to blast us like hitting a sleeping breld. And our prey did nothing but run. So why are we here, and the drone is spinning around in a swarl? We need to know, because that's going to tell us how we survive when the others find us."

"You're right." There was a pause, and Dex fancied that his ship's artificial intelligence was heaving a sigh. Even without such an emotional outburst, the delay concerned him. How much damage had the processors taken?

Before he could form his fear into words, Santiago spoke. "I'm calling up the telemetry from the battle and will compare this drone's capabilities with what we know about the relics we've captured in the Disk. We've never given much thought to the weapons systems. I will have to check my archives for information."

"Ask Scarlet; she went through that military history phase. Remember those war games she and... Who was that straw-haired disaster we apprenticed?"

"Gary Client. Sharp mind; entirely clumsy with my systems. Always daydreamed when something didn't interest him. He did enjoy war gaming...the tactics, at any rate."

"Well, that's what we need, tactics. Get on it. Get Scarlet to help you."

"Dex, remember when we are."

He shook his head. "Her files, dammit. Her files! Now leave me alone while I work out this interface."

Nonetheless, he had to steel himself against the pang, as strong as that day so long ago, when he remembered anew that his wife was dead.

It only took him a few more minutes to get the interface working to the best of its ability. The commands felt clumsy and the sensors not nearly as refined as he was used to (despite Scarlet's declarations that the vids always felt so real), but it was better than sitting in the kitchen watching his life be bandied about by two ships on a computer screen.

He pulled off the cap and gloves and set them on the mangled but semi-working console, then went into the kitchen. He needed to think, to pit his human, hunter's mind against the challenges that lay ahead; and as long as he was doing that, he might as well do it while the medical chair worked on his body. He'd just finished his next swipe with the bone knitter and was working on his second cup of coffee when Santiago contacted him.

"Our victory," Santiago started without preamble, "came about because of surprise and unusual technology. Look."

Upon the kitchen screen, a schematic of a drone appeared, one more detailed than he'd seen before. Lines of blue and yellow outlined its systems; he recognized the blue as systems they'd known from years of studying the relics. Yellow must have been what Santiago had gleaned from its studies of the ship in battle.

"We've always been aware that the drones were equipped with multiple lasers, which were assumed to be weapons."

"Assumed?" Dex asked. They'd seemed damned effective as weapons to him.

"I will not deny their usefulness in the offensive," Santiago replied, as the schematic became dotted, then littered with arrows pointing to laser turrets that covered the drone from all sides. "However, I found it odd that, given the maneuverability of the drones under normal circumstances, that they should have so many lasers with such coverage, especially when the torpedo bays are fore and aft."

"They had torpedoes? Thank God that they've expended them by now."

"We should probably not assume that, though it seems highly likely. I am speculating on the torpedo bays based on what we've learned from our own captured ship. Its nose and tail are almost entirely devoted to torpedoes. We have seen smaller, similar areas in the drone relics we've captured, but the accepted theory was that the designated areas were in fact for escape pods for the crew. I now propose that there have never been any living crews to need such equip-ment—nor have there been for any of the relics found."

"But we've dated those relics," Dex pro-tested. "Some of them are centuries old, subjective to themselves."

"Indeed. But it also answers the question of why their communications are so rudi-mentary."

"Elomij, what happened to your people?" Dex muttered. He ran one hand over his face, barely registering the scraggly growth. "Nev-er mind, we'll deal with that later. Are there torpedoes in our prey?"

"Not aft if I am reading the schematics correctly, and it would stand to reason that if it had torpedoes, it would have used them against us. However, the forward port side torpedo bays have taken irreparable dam-age. If there are any left, they would be there. Why? What do you plan?"

"Just listing assets at this point. So what's all this tell you about the lasers?"

"My guess, based on what I've been able to glean from Gary's Starship Marauders game, is that the lasers were primarily in-tended for point defense, which makes sense given the environment they are battling in. Observe."

On the screen, the diagram of the drone shrunk, and a map of the area they were traversing imposed itself around it. The drone fired a laser. For a moment, the red line on the display traversed a fairly straight line, but after a certain distance, it began to curve wildly.

"So, they can only hit close up?"

"Purposely, at any rate," Santiago answered. "It also explains why they came so close before firing."

"But they've battled in this spacetime insanity for centuries! Why haven't they adapted?"

"I do not believe they can, and for the same reason as they have no escape pods. No people."

Dex grunted thoughtfully. "No one to tell them to do it differently?"

"Or, more likely, no one left to design new targeting systems, which is why my paltry cutting laser inflicted more steady damage than its weapons-grade ones. I know how to map and adapt the changing gravity gradients. I also discovered that its shields, and that of the Civilization B ship we have captured, have the effect of smoothing the gravitational fluxes; thus, the wake I have been able to slide us into. My shields, however, do not have the same effect, and it took several shots before it found a smooth spot generated by our own CivB shield."

"So we weren't hit when the CivB shield went offline?"

"No. Quite the opposite: the CivB shield went offline as a result of the 'lucky' shot."

"All right." Succumbing to a sudden urge to move, he pushed himself out of the med chair and went to the coffee maker to pour himself a cup. "All right. So we've got the advantage of surprise and some superior targeting. What other assets do we have?"

"You," Santiago said immediately.

"Me?"

"You...and to a lesser extent, me as well. The drones are limited in their programming, carrying only the knowledge of how Civilization B ships have always fought. We are not only a wild card in their calculations, but we both are able to innovate and adapt." He paused before saying, "I do not know how to calculate how much that changes the odds of our survival, but we have performed feats that defy statistical probability before."

"That we have." Dex chuckled as he studied the deep brown liquid in his mug. "But we always do it by being smarter, by thinking three steps ahead of 'statistical possibility.'

Status of our injured prey? And I don't just mean changes. What did that repair robot tell you?"

"It was a specialized bot, Dex, with a single mission: care for the backup shield generator. It was simple luck that it came across the scout bot and then moved to investigate the hole you'd cut into the hull."

"Is the other generator broken?"

"Unknown, but it would stand to reason that it still functions since it—and we—are still here."

He swirled the coffee in his cup, thinking. "True, without the shields, it'd have been torn into so many strings of quantum elements by now. And it also stands to reason that unless some other bot is fixing it, we just killed its backup."

Outside, the patient, red-shifted light made its ponderous way to the window as matter and energy splashed over the shields with force as destructive as the pull of the singularity. He suspected that angular momentum kept them from falling in, and for that, they were depending on their prey. Even without the threat of other drones, they were running out of time.

Time. A gruff laugh escaped his throat. How much time had passed in his reality?

Had they lost decades or centuries...maybe even a millennium?

He stared out the window, letting his subconscious work while his conscious mind went numb. Forgotten, his coffee cooled. Santiago recognized his mood and remained silent as it made its own calculations.

"How do we get out of here?" Dex finally asked, though the answer was already forming in his mind.

"Presumably the same way we got here."

"No. The way *that ship* got out of here the first time. The way those drones are escaping the influence of that singularity to come after us now. Just like they have special shielding to survive this chaos, they must have a special drive to escape it. It's the only thing that makes sense."

"Then why have we not found those drives in the relics we've recovered?" Santiago asked.

"How would we know? So much of the relics have been burned out. They're always floating among the detritus... all except this ship, Santiago. This ship alone has escaped intact, and that's how it had eluded us for so long. It wasn't just following the swarls. It was hiding. But why? Why escape?"

"The pod of drones we saw," Santiago answered. "Their course seemed too targeted for a relic. I didn't mention it at the time because we weren't going after them. Dex, if they were powered and others caught them..."

"Nothing we can do about that now," Dex said. "Keep an eye out for human ships if you want, but most likely anyone else would have let them go at the first sign of trouble."

"That is true."

Dex felt a spark of reassurance to hear the droll twist in Santiago's voice. He replied, "Crossing with us the first time almost destroyed us; so why hasn't it tried to cross again to finish us off? What's preventing it? Where's it dragging us now?"

"It continues ahead, although it has angled away from the singularity. And no, I cannot tell you what lies ahead of us."

Dex nodded, thinking. "We need to fix that. Get something on its hull, put a sensor package in front of its nose. I don't care how you do it, but I want to know what's coming, and I want to influence the direction of that ship as much as we can. Now, what about behind? No drones coming from below?"

"Not yet."

"Give me an estimate."

"If there were drones ready to receive the message, and if they started immediately upon getting the transmission, and if the Disk we are in is similar to our own Disk, I would say, two to four hours."

Not as much time as he'd like, but better than nothing. He slammed down the last of his cold, bitter drink and from habit, placed the cup in the washing drawer. "The robots inside that ship don't see in the visual spectrum. Can you modify my suit to make me look like something innocuous or to blend in with the surroundings?"

"Perhaps," came Santiago's cautious reply. "Blending in would be easier; you already have shown that they will ignore you if you are out of the way and still, as when you first ambushed the repair bot. But why are you returning to the ship?"

"There's only one reason that I can think of for that ship not pulling us back across the event horizon. Something in there is broken and isn't getting repaired, or isn't getting repaired fast enough. If that's the case, I'm going in and giving it a hand."

"You don't know what you're doing," Santiago observed, and again, Dex found himself touched and irritated at the worried tone of Santiago's digital voice.

"You're right, but I didn't really know what I was doing with the CivB generator we have. Still, I can recognize a broken piece when I see one, and I'll have you to help."

"Me?"

"You may have to romance that ship, my friend."

Chapter Ten

Hudon Takes a New Consort

Hudon had stormed away from Elomij, his fury heating his steps so that they burned into the Bloody Road. Where his footsteps incinerated the path, none could live to fight. The People mourned the loss of battle-grounds until one said, "Let us create automatons and send them into the desolation. There they shall carry our wrath to our brothers." So they created great machines which needed neither flesh nor blood, food nor drink, consciousness nor passion. With minds shaped only for battle, the constructs set forth and brought a new shade of glory to the Bloody Road. And when Hudon looked back and saw his steps filling with that glory, he was amused, and the People basked in the glow of his pride.

Soon, however, he found himself lonely, for greatly did he enjoy strolling with Elomij and sharing with her the wonders of their handiwork. He could not return to the goddess of beauty and change. No, she had responded to his boasts with yawns, demanded to seek other trails, then spurned the advances she'd enjoyed for so long. Like her name, the goddess of change was too fickle for Hudon, and so he bundled his desires into a great storm.

"Go!" he said to the wild winds of his yearning. "Retrieve for me a consort charmed with inevitability and permanence. For I, Hudon, God of War, demand a more suitable mate." Hudon breathed upon the storm and sent it racing across the Might Have Been and to the Eternal Fields. And, wearied from his efforts, he settled against a tree growing from the Might Have Been and slept. As he slept, the storms returned and invaded his dreams. He had visions of one who gave a gift both feared and sought after, which comforted the receiver while grieving those around him. A gift that all received, and none could return.

When he awoke, he looked into the dark, eternal eyes of Corsha, the goddess of death.

"I am not confident in this plan," Santiago told Dex.

"Meaning it's probably going to fail?" Dex sucked hard on the bag of dawlsu to get the last of the spicy meat paste, then tossed the empty container aside. He'd need the nourishment, and in case Santiago's worst fears came true, he'd at least gotten his favorite food for a last meal. He'd also made a pot of his best coffee, now in a second sipping bag in his spacesuit. With a recharged medical bracelet and his spectacles in place, he was ready to suit up.

"Meaning I cannot predict a probability one way or another. There are too many factors involved, including certain wild cards."

Dex snorted as he stepped into the suit with his good leg then eased the injured one in. The multiple treatments with the bone knitter had repaired the breaks, but the bones were still weak. "We 'wild cards' are what's going to make this plan work. You'll have to trust in human intuition this time."

"Scarlet's intuition had greater success."

Dex paused, one arm in the sleeve of the suit, and smiled. "Yeah, she had a knack. But she's gone now, old friend, so we'll have to do with hunter's instincts."

"With respect, your 'hunter's instincts' are telling you to put our repair bots and my cognitive systems in peril."

Dex bent down, stuck the other arm into the left sleeve, then straightened, pulling the suit on over his head. It smoothed into place with familiar reassurance as he ran his hands over the waistline, joining shirt and pants. He checked the equipment on his belt, making sure the tether lines were secure. "We could do nothing and wait to die."

"No, thank you."

"Then quit whining. You're sure about my stealth shield?"

Santiago had reprogrammed the suit to mimic the readings behind him and project them in front, and visa-versa. If he stood still with his back against a wall, he should become essentially invisible to the casual alien observer. "As sure as I can be. We will know more when you test it out—which will be on the captured ship. Hopefully, if there are any kinks, I can straighten them out remotely before it recognizes you and shoots you."

"I trust you."

"And I am trusting you, Dex. I may be an artificial intelligence, but I do value my existence. And our friendship. Be careful and be ready to return at a moment's notice if I detect drones approaching."

"Yes, Mother. Did you download the map?"

"Yes. Your screen will take you first to the torpedo bays because they are on the way to the drive system."

Dex slung his relic gun over his shoulder. "Good. Be ready with the cargo bots. If I see any torpedoes, we'll retrieve them; maybe we can use them as mines. Set them out, blast them with a laser when a drone gets near."

"That is probably the least effective use of them. However, if they have seeking technology and we can activate them, that might prove most helpful."

"Either way, have those bots ready when I call—and you'd better stealth them, too. We already lost one spybot to that alien ship's sentinels. Of course, it'd be easier for all of us if you could just convince that ship that we're in this together."

"You tax my abilities, Dex. Being able to convince a repair bot that our CivB generator was its designated back-up is one thing. Convincing a warship that we are allies is a very different endeavor."

"You haven't been challenged enough lately." When Santiago did not reply, he added, "Unless you have a better idea?"

"None with a better chance of success than your intuition."

Dex slid on his gloves, twisting the wrists to secure the nanofiber connections. He grabbed his helmet and headed to the airlock. "Let's get on with it, then."

On the way, however, he paused. Again listening to his instincts, he returned to the shipping crate Molly had sent them. A repair bot rested in the foam, hooked to the still-packed recharging station. It was a little over half-charged. He grabbed it and stuck it in his pouch.

While the computer depressurized the airlock, he looked at the portal that opened into the docking tube. Designed for medical emergencies where someone might have to be carried or carted out, it allowed two humans to walk abreast through it. Still. He gnawed on his lip. "If we find torpedoes, will they fit?"

"I am prepared to remove the docking tube and open the cargo hatch if not," Santiago replied. "The pulley is still in place, and the backup computer is programmed to handle the transfer either way."

"All right, then." He opened the door and pushed off. The creamy color of the oblong tube seemed unnaturally bright and clean after the dinginess of the *Santiago's* wrecked interior. For some reason, it made him feel even more exposed than if he'd traversed the vacuum of space between the two ships. It didn't help that he moved not toward light or the reassurance of a familiar station, but to the aching blackness of an alien ship—a warship, at that. He shrugged off the feeling as he entered the darkness.

His suit automatically switched to radar, and he experienced a fleeting surge of vertigo before he again adjusted to the oddly strobing images. He flattened himself against the wall as he readied himself. He called up the map, checked his route, and took a careful survey of his surroundings. Here, as outside the ship, a couple of bots he'd zapped floated inert—or were they just waiting for new commands after failing to repair the hole he'd created? They hadn't bothered with the docking tube; did they accept it as a useful substitute? Whatever the reason, he should count his blessings and move on.

The corridor he was in circumnavigated the ship, nose to tail. It was large, larger than any bot he'd seen so far would need to move around. They must have used it for moving equipment. Torpedoes, too? He took note of the walls around him, all bearing a uniform pattern of holes in which the robots would stick their jagged feet, before returning his attention back down the straight, clear path. He braced his feet against the wall and pushed off hard, sending himself flying to the far end of the ship. He knew he'd lose reaction time should he need to plaster himself against a wall to avoid an approaching bot, but he felt he made up for it by not causing vibrations in the floor from his magnetic boots engaging and disengaging on the metal. His gamble paid off. The few bots he saw moved over and around him, oblivious or unconcerned.

He laughed to himself. *Weren't expecting this, were you? And why should you, when you've never come up against a living, thinking man?*

He felt a flare of hope so strong that it took his breath away. He would continue to live—precisely because he was a thinking being. He could adapt; he could change; he could win.

He would win.

A robot passed him by, silent and uncaring, apparently programmed to ignore anything that didn't pose a direct threat. Intent on its mission, the same mission it had been fulfilling for God-knew how long.

Had the People been the same way, moving from conflict to habit to instinct, ignoring the changes—the carnage—until it was simply how things had always been? Had they traveled mindlessly into oblivion with the same inevitability of their spaghettified systems spiraling into the singularity? Had there been no Dokuchaev zones in their entire history, when they had a moment of stability to stop and wonder why they were so intent on slitting their brothers' throats? Did they hate so much?

Or did they hate at all? Hudon's words came back to him from when he'd told the god he'd hunted both the People and the Worthy Foe: "Is there a difference?" And the myths of the Elomij, if they indeed related to their ancient roots in this system, never differentiated between races. They were brothers and foes, choosing to place victory over everything, even their own survival.

Is that what I did? Am I in this mess because I was too stubborn to put my own life and Santiago's safety ahead of victory over some artifact?

The map on his faceplate signaled his next turn. Time enough later to examine his conscience. Right now, he needed to survive—and that meant defeating the drones that were on their way to destroy this ship and them with it. He needed a victory, or at least a draw that would allow them to escape.

He caught the corner of the junction, stopping his forward progress, then flipped himself forward and up until his back was pressed against the wall of the corridor above him. Even in zero G, his muscles strained to perform the unaccustomed acrobatics. He paused, listening to the rasping of his own breathing, loud in his suit, and feeling for vibrations that might suggest he had been noticed.

A slow count to sixty, and no sign of discovery. Dex eased himself away from the wall and surveyed the cavernous bay.

He hissed at what he saw. And he thought Santiago's damage was bad.

The outer wall, curved and bearing five tubes to deliver destruction upon its enemy, had been blown in by some force—a near miss of an enemy torpedo, or perhaps a kamikaze effort by an attacking drone. Whatever the case, the trips across the event horizon had played havoc with the structure, twisting and warping the metal so that it bulged along some lines, thinned and cracked on others. It brought to mind the bizarre wrinkles and growths on Scarlet's body, where the sickly areas of accelerated aging met the healthy tissue.

He shivered and fought against the memory of taking one gnarled hand and pressing it against his lips. His beautiful Scarlet...

"Dex, you've been very quiet," Santiago's voice pulled him from his flight of dark fancy.

"So've you," he rejoined with a growl. "I'm in the torpedo bay. It's a mess. None of the tubes are going to be any use. Like we expected." A sudden spasm of sympathy for the damaged ship washed over him. His throat tightened, his hands balled into fists, and his eyes squeezed shut.

"What about the torpedoes?" Santiago asked.

Dex shook himself. What's past is past. He had to concentrate on the present; on getting them away safely so they might have a future. He pulled his gaze from the twisted hull and scanned the rest of the room. "A few exploded in here. I'm seeing torn metal, damaged bots... Looks like they gave up on this section a long time ago." He set the magnets on his boots to minimum and let them pull him to the deck. He started forward and to the right, stepping lightly.

The gross deformation of the hull bulged, making the bay seem smaller than it in fact was. He noted it enough to be sure it was holding, then moved on. For now, he needed to concentrate on the area toward the interior of the ship. The radar of his helmet outlined the scene in stark shades of grays. Here, the damage was less than near the hull, though that didn't say as much as he'd have liked.

Long rails led from the innermost part of the ship to the hull—or would have, if they'd not been twisted, torn, and blasted apart by the chaos of battles and escapes. He could easily see that several torpedoes had sat upon the rails, waiting for launch or in the process of being launched, their detonations destroying not only themselves, but the torpedoes around them. If he was going to find anything, it would be closer to the interior. He reported this to Santiago and turned his back to the hull.

He found one robot with thick, muscular arms to complement its spindlier ones, laying on its side near what looked like an intact torpedo. He paused to take hold of his relic gun before cautiously approaching the bot. He nudged it with his toe. It rocked, although the feet still stuck in the crevices of the floor kept it from floating away. It did not respond.

He looked over the torpedo. The casing seemed intact, and the systems dead. That suited him just fine.

"Bring in the bots, Santiago. I found one."

"Just one? Is it worth the risk?"

"Cool your thrusters; I'm still looking. Besides, if we don't take risks now, we're assured failure later."

"True enough, but they should be calculated risks."

Dex laughed at what had become an old joke between them. "Let me know when you can calculate them, then."

"Unfortunately, once you enter the equation, all calculations are meaningless."

"You need an upgrade." He pulled out marker tape and placed an X on the torpedo. The cargo bot would seek out the mark and carry it back to the ship. Then he stepped carefully around the presumed-dead bot and moved toward the next rail.

"In that we agree. Any more torpedoes? I have the cargo bot prepared."

"Have it float down the middle of the corridor. The bots here completely ignored me."

The next rail was intact toward the interior, but empty. Had they expended all the torpedoes in this line, then? He moved on and found another torpedo, this one without a robotic escort, and another beyond that. He marked them and reported them to Santiago, his mind still on the empty rail.

"That's it. Five rails, three torpedoes."

"Understood. You should see an opening between the third and fourth rail. That corridor will lead you to the engine room."

"Right. Just want to check one thing. That empty rail bothers me for some reason. Call it instinct."

"We've used up an hour already. We do not have a lot of time to indulge your instincts."

"I only want a minute." He returned to the rail, standing not far from the exit, and looked it over. The clamps holding the torpedoes in place had not been released so much as sheared off. "That's curious."

"Thirty seconds, Dex."

"Nag, nag." He followed the line of the rail, his attention focused on how it thinned and elongated, until he saw a torpedo captured in the hull, as if the skin of the ship had stretched and torn, only to heal itself around the bomb. He pulled out a sounder from his belt and pressed it against the rippled metal. He hooted.

"What do you see, Dex?"

"I see a good place to blast a hole."

Chapter Eleven

"Be careful!" Santiago warned. "We don't know how well that shield will hold."

"I aim to find out. Don't worry." Setting the sounder back in its place, he pulled out the small tube of cutting putty he'd brought with him. He hadn't expected something like this but had brought it in case Santiago's estimates of what he could crawl through weren't as accurate as during his last visit. He did not want a repeat of last time, especially adding getting stuck or leaving something vital behind. The putty was faster acting than the industrial stuff, but he only had the one tube. He hoped it'd be enough.

When he'd described the thin line in the hull around the torpedo, he upped the magnetism of his boots, just in case, and waited.

The putty cut through the metal easily, leaving a thin line of emptiness. He switched to the visual spectrum and saw the halo-like circle illuminating the torpedo in dim light. He planted his feet securely and shoved at the tail of the torpedo. It sailed forward, spinning end over end, and when it approached the shield, the shield cracked and spread just large enough to allow it to pass through.

"Yes! Santiago, get a couple of bots making three thruster packs and send them over with whatever they need to attach the packs to the torpedoes. We're going to re-arm this ship."

Switching back to radar and turning away from the hole, he clumped his way toward the exit, chuckling. No machine calculations could ever outdo Dex Hollister and his instincts.

"Bots instructed and working. You need to hurry to our next objective. I've just detected several drones en route from the singularity."

"Already?" He eased the magnetism on his boots and picked up the pace. "What happened to two to four hours?"

"I did say it was an estimate."

He got to the entrance, saw the narrower but clear corridor, and launched himself. "Can you revise it now?" He didn't bother to keep the exasperation out of his voice.

"Perhaps an hour to contact. I have been attempting to access the alien ship's controls—without success. I have not made it past its security protocols. I do not have time to learn to 'romance' the control systems of that ship."

Dex swore. The empty hall moved past him in a blur, but not fast enough.

"Not helpful," Santiago said. "What's our Plan B? Take the left!"

Dex flung out an arm and caught the junction he nearly missed in his distraction. The momentum yanked at his shoulder, making him hiss with pain, but he caught himself and weaseled his way through the cramped, machine-filled space. Only a little father to the main engines. What then?

"Scarlet, got any ideas? I could use a little *woman's intuition* right now!"

"Scarlet is dead, Dex."

"I know!" he snarled, though his heart pounded because for a fleeting second, he'd felt she was alive, on the *Santiago*, biting her beautiful lip and racking her beautiful brains for a way to save them all. In that moment, he'd realized just how alone he felt. Loneliness closing in, just like the corridor...

"Talk to me, Dex," Santiago urged.

"Leave me alone. I'm concentrating!" This part of the ship had taken damage despite its being farther from the nose. Loose equipment hung in his way, forcing him to shove it aside or worm his way around. The images on his faceplate confused him, as everything seemed to crowd in on him.

Oh, he hated cramped places. Like the time he and his brothers got caught in a storm and he'd gotten left behind and had holed up in a cave, only the cave was more dirt than rock and the heavy rains caused it to cave in...

He clawed his way forward, his hands slipping, mud getting in his nose and eyes...

Focus, Dex!

His bracelet tingled. He pushed ahead. Cave-in or alien ship, he had to keep pushing ahead.

His mind cleared by the time he got to the control room. He paused at the entrance, head down, banishing images and fears of being buried alive, forcing his breathing to slow.

"I'm here," he told Santiago, then looked up.

The tangled mess he'd just clawed through was apparently a hint of the damage he'd find in central engineering. Something had exploded...maybe the weapons control, not that it mattered; whatever it was had sent its shrapnel across the bubble-shaped room. He saw pieces of metal planted in equipment like ax blades in a tree; one machine whose function he couldn't fathom had cracked like an egg, complete with some kind of goo, frozen in the act of pouring itself out. Bots apparently assigned to handle the repairs floated among the wreckage or hung loosely from the walls, as dead as the equipment they were intended to save.

Dex didn't even have the energy to swear.

"Santiago, you see this?"

"The ship's been depending on backup systems," Santiago concluded.

"But we killed its shield generator. Why has it not spaghettified?" He pulled himself out of the tight squeeze of the corridor and floated, careful not to tear his suit on the wreckage. He searched for the generator, for something that looked like a drive system, for anything that looked like it might be functioning, but with limited knowledge and no exterior cues of lights and status panels to indicate activity, he was lost.

"There must be a tertiary system. Or perhaps it has some other kind of resistance we don't know about, but that can only take limited strain."

Dex grunted. "Could be why it's not moved from the straight path. I found the broken generator. Vac, what a mess."

"I see it. Are you trying to salvage some parts?"

Dex answered by pulling out a cutting tool and applying it to the hulk. "Check the records from that hunk of junk you romanced earlier and tell me what parts it needs. Then find me the fastest way to the backup room and revive that repair bot. If it's still able to function, it's got work to do."

Since he didn't have to worry about damaging other systems, and with Santiago's knowledge from the repair bot to guide him, he made quick work of the inert shield generator and had filled a bag with spares. There were several parts the backup needed, most of which were (he hoped) in working condition.

"Why didn't it cannibalize this thing earlier?" Dex grumbled.

"For the same reason I would not have cut a hole in the ship's hull to throw torpedoes through," Santiago replied. "It would not have occurred to its programming. Incidentally, our repair bots have added the thrusters, and the cargo bot has them in position. Shall I return the bots to me?"

"Leave the cargo bot in case it has to push those bombs out. Bring a couple of bots to me. They can haul this bag of parts to the backup room. Any luck talking to our 'friend'?"

"It is 'conscious,' but unable to move. The drones are on an intercept course. We do not have much time—perhaps thirty minutes, though I would not bet our lives on it."

"If it can tell you it's damage, relay that to a repair bot. We need to get it moving again. What about the engines?"

Santiago replied by putting up a target node. He followed the node until he was facing the engines. Even though everything around them was so much torn metal, the drive system looked intact.

"Is it shielded?" he demanded.

"Unknown. That is beyond the need to know of the repair bot I 'romanced,' and I am unable to communicate with the ship itself."

Dex reached out with a finger and gingerly nudged a floating bot toward the engines. A handspan from impacting the drive system, it bounced.

That's what he thought. Even if it were broken, even if he knew enough to fix it, there was no way to reach it. He'd have to trust.

Two repair bots floated through the tunnel he'd traversed earlier. He attached the bag to them, got the route from Santiago, and pushed on to the backup.

Again, he paused at the entrance, this time of the secondary engineering room, and scanned the room. Unlike the frenetic activity of before, the bots in the room were mostly inert, latched onto floor, walls, and ceiling near what he supposed was their equipment of responsibility, waiting for system failure to spur them into action. The only exceptions were the repair bots still at work on the damage caused by their own over-excited offense against Dex, and the dead robot Santiago had shanghaied, still floating not far from the generator they'd vandalized for spare parts. He saw a smaller bot also floating inert. One of its arms had been torn off. Was that the one that shot at him? If so, it was a good sign, as far as he was concerned.

"Looks pretty peaceful," Dex told Santiago, his voice low even though nothing would hear him outside the suit. "Think they've learned their lesson about shooting in their own engine room?"

"Possible. Our damaged 'friend' does not know, however, and I would suggest that we make no assumptions. They may deem you a greater danger than the damage of their own lasers."

Dex grunted. "Under normal circumstances, they'd be right, but we need each other now. There any way you can convince our 'friend' into telling the others we're here to help?"

"I am trying. I suggest you send one of our bots in first to work on it."

"And see if they'll accept an alien's help in making repairs. Just what I was thinking."

Dex eased his relic gun from around his back and settled it into his hands. He felt a flash of gratitude for the weapon, especially its easy button trigger and internal target adjustments. Even in a spacesuit and on the run, it allowed him to point and shoot, and the internal workings had made the adjustments necessary to ensure it hit the targets. This time, he had even greater control, and (relatively speaking) the luxury of time. Tying the weapon's sights to his faceplate, he swept the area with the scope, pausing to note the bots that might be targets. If it came down to a fight this time, the gun would identify and aim automatically at the targets, even if he pointed it blindly behind his back and fired. Should he face another wildly scurrying horde, it would set a wider beam and fire.

He'd survived the wild chase once. He didn't want to push his luck any more than he had to.

Thus prepared, he unlatched the bag from his repair bots, then set himself in as comfortable a position as he could and pointed the gun into the room. "Okay, Santiago. Send in one of our bots."

The round bot fired its tiny thrusters and floated in.

Dex watched, moving from eye to scope, as it neared the broken bot and hovered. When nothing happened, narrow arms unfolded from its globe-shaped body; slowly, as his father might have when approaching a wild beast, reaching into his pack carefully to pull out a knife to free it from some poacher's trap or to get a sedative to calm it for treatment or transport. He could almost hear the bot whispering reassurances and found himself muttering as well. "Easy, now. We're not here to hurt you..."

The bot extended an arm. Dex hefted the gun; waited.

The bot touched the broken machine without any reaction from it or the other robots around it.

As if that first contact gave it confidence, his repair bot moved quickly, removing the busted and burned panel, making expert strokes with a solvent-laced brush to clean away the scorching, and working, presumably at Santiago's control, and with direction from the inured bot itself, to repair or bypass damaged systems. He gave it a few minutes to ensure that none of the other bots were simply biding their time before swooping in for an attack, but the other robots continued their own duties or waited, powered-down and motionless.

"How long until that thing is up and repairing the shield generator?" Dex demanded.

"The damage is worse than it estimated. It has no control over its own limbs," Santiago replied. "Our bot is attempting bypasses—like rerouting nerves. The drones will be in range before we are finished."

Dex swore. "Then you'd better make it convince the others that they have no choice but to take our help."

He shouldered his weapon and snatched up the bag of spare parts.

"Dex!"

"You got an alternative?" When Santiago didn't reply, he pushed in, the second repair bot at his side. Despite his nerves screaming for him to make haste, he moved easily, eyes constantly roving, looking for any sign of unwanted reaction. Nothing acknowledged his presence or moved in challenge as he got to the broken generator.

He spoke a few commands, and the faceplate visuals split, with a 360-degree view of the room making a thin strip along the top, and the rest narrowing in on the damaged shield generator. He felt a flare of optimism as he surveyed the damage. The overtaxed system had shorted out in several places, causing overloads in others as the unchallenged energy found its own outlet. Figured that he'd find in this generator the same flaws he saw in his own. It oddly reassured him as well; if the aliens hadn't found a way around their own machine's design flaw, how could he be expected to have done so with his own stolen generator?

Even better; he might not understand it, but he did know how to fix it—or at least to jury-rig it back into operation. He clipped one end of the bag to his belt and pulled it open.

"How much time?"

"Twenty minutes, perhaps. That's including the time you'll need to return."

"Vac! As soon as that bot is ready to make repairs, get it up here. Don't worry about fixing it totally; just whatever it needs to work."

He sighted in on the first broken piece he came to, a twisty, cylindrical object Scarlet had dubbed "the rockaby." It connected to several other systems through simple plugs and (when working) rotated sixty degrees one way, then the other, for reasons Scarlet hadn't even been able to guess at. This rockaby sported half a dozen holes where the sockets had burst, and its normally smooth shape bubbled, giving evidence to smaller internal explosions.

Dex grabbed a spanner and reached in, removing the plugs still attached, and checking each. By some miracle, only two were damaged. He might be able to bend them into workable shape. A couple were close enough that he could ease them out for his repair bot to work on while he removed the damaged piece and set it floating in place beside him while he took its replacement from the bag.

He tightened the joins and had started to search for the next piece when the ship suddenly lurched. His spanner banged against one of the other plugs, and only the fact that he, by reflex, had released it prevented him from creating another short between the two systems. "What was that?" he demanded.

"The ship's accelerating. I think it has finally spotted the drones."

He blinked sweat from his eyes and went back to plugging wires into the rocker. "Course?"

"Straight ahead. I think it means to outrun them, but even with time dilation in our favor, it won't win. Dex, it's time to return home."

He found the next broken piece, reached in with his spanner. "Without this ship shielded and pulling us free, we don't have a chance."

"Without you in here helping me fight off these drones, we don't have a chance."

A section of his helmet started to flash red. He saw the repair bot being lifted by his own. "Can it take over?" he asked Santiago.

"I'm going to give it control of our repair bots to assist. I've only been able to restore control to two of its arms. You need to hook it in place so it can work."

"Two arms?" he protested as he moved aside, grasped a leg, and fitted it into a hole, wiggling inexpertly until he could no longer yank it back out. "Will that be enough?"

"And how many arms do you have? Get over here, Dex."

As if to underscore Santiago's urgency, the ship again shifted around him. He grabbed another leg, jammed it in with quicker success, then repeated it once more. Around him, the alien repair bots came to life, apparently called to action by the ship in anticipation of battle damage. "You'd better be right," he said.

"Now you must trust my programming. Hurry." A schematic appeared on his helmet, showing him the fastest way back to the docking tube.

Dex twisted in the direction of the exit, planted a foot against the wall behind him and shoved off—just as a repair bot pushed itself off another area of the wall. Unable to halt his motion, Dex did the only thing he could—pulled his arms in and made himself straight to hit the machine with his hard helmet.

They collided.

He hit the smaller, slower bot and jerked his neck, flinging it out of his way, then stretched out his arms in an attempt to correct his trajectory or to grab at the wall and push himself into the junction if he missed. He started to pray that the bot would ignore the interruption to its route, then discarded the idea. His God would do what He willed; and with Hudon as their god, he could count on the bot's reaction.

Sure enough, a quick glance up at the rear view on his faceplate showed that bot and two others turning their attention to him.

He didn't waste air swearing. He just grabbed the lip of the junction and shoved himself down the corridor. A new route traced itself on his faceplate—through the tight corridors.

"Have I got time for that?" he demanded to Santiago.

The ship shifted to port around him and shook.

"The drones are firing at the alien ship. Two direct hits," Santiago reported.

In front of Dex, a piece of the bulkhead flared where a laser from the repair bots pursuing him ignited a wall. He reached out with a hand and slapped the hull, changing his vector and increasing his speed. Reaching under his arm, he grabbed the relic gun and shot blindly behind him, grateful now that he'd taken those few moments earlier to program in the targets. "Vac the long way—show me the fast route."

The original lines returned to his faceplate. "Don't get killed," Santiago warned.

Throwing up a shoulder, he twisted his body to again add a randomness to his path. He was rewarded by another flare on the bulkhead, signifying a miss. He saw his first turn, reached up and snagged the edge. He pulled himself up, braced his feet against a small panel whose function he didn't know and didn't care about, and pushed.

Pain flared up his leg.

Dex screamed. The whole world went white, then gray. Dimly, he heard someone calling his name, but he couldn't catch a breath to answer. He gritted his teeth and panted, still moving forward, but helpless to do anything else.

Then his brother Brade was yelling at him to stop being a weakling, and his father was urging him. Scarlet reached out her hand.

He reached for her...

His hand closed on some outcropping. Natural? Mechanical? He didn't know; the world had blurred. It didn't matter. He had to keep moving. For Brade. For Scarlet. For Santiago. For himself. He pulled himself up, then flung himself forward.

The world started to clear, and he heard Santiago shout a direction to him just in time to fling himself to the left of a fork in corridors.

"Got it!" he gasped.

"Dex, are you all right?"

"I broke my vaccing leg again. Of course, I'm not all right! What's going on out there?" Anger brought clarity and, ignoring his throbbing right leg, he started to jerk and twist again.

"Seven drones surrounding the ship. They've ignored me so far, but they are punching holes in the shields of the ship."

"And what are you doing about it?"

"They aren't targeting me, and I don't want to draw attention to myself until you are aboard."

"Vac that! Fire. We can't let them destroy this ship."

"If they hit the docking tube..."

An alarm in his suit cut off Santiago's transmission as something shoved him sideways. Suit tear!

"I've been hit! Left arm." He again grabbed his gun and shot backward as his suit continued with alarms and complaints. A pressure cuff tightened on his arm above the tear, preventing his air from leaking out further. The entire suit cooled as more heat was poured into the left arm to protect his flesh from exposure to vacuum.

He fired three more times, then dropped the gun and grabbed the wall with his right hand to propel himself faster. A quick glance at his rear view showed two bots floating inert. He hoped the ship wouldn't need them, but it was its own fault.

"Fire on those drones! Got a torpedo ready? Shoot it once I get to the docking tube. Might buy us some time."

"Understood. Firing lasers. Disengaging a capture beam from the ship to use against a drone. One more turn, Dex, and you are there. How is your suit?"

"Dandy, thanks!" Indicators were flashing red—minutes of air left; suit still leaking; heat draining. His arm throbbed from having its circulation cut. His leg had mercifully gone from white-hot agony to mere pain. The change in direction from the suit leak and from firing the relic gun had slowed him. Worse was the funny, disoriented feeling he was starting to get.

Shock. He could deal with the pain, but not shock.

He latched onto his anger, used it as a club to beat away the numbness. "You will not win. Do you hear me, Hudon? Victory is mine today!"

"I have a drone in capture. Applying shock beam. Dex, I'm hit!"

"Keep zapping it. Taking the last turn. What about the torpedo?" He saw the docking tube swaying slightly as Santiago fought to hold position in the battle. The airlock on the other side gaped open and inviting. He propelled himself one-handed toward it, ignoring the shakes and how very slow he seemed to move.

"Ready. Drone disabled. Repelling it and selecting new target."

Just a few more feet. It looked so good on the other side. Familiar. Safe. He laughed. Safe? His left foot bumped the wall. He paused, bending his knee.

"I'm being fired upon."

"Launch the torpedo."

He shoved himself into the docking tube.

The tube glowed with the explosions of battle. He concentrated on the airlock beyond.

A flash of light and heat he could feel even through his spacesuit, and the gabrium/titanium nanoweave ripped like foil beside him. The pressure of the laser caused it to sway, but he twisted into the curve and shot past before the flowing wall caught him. His back bumped against the swaying tube and he grasped a bracer and pushed again.

He slammed into the far wall of airlock and saw the doors slide shut as the world around him grayed.

"Dex!" Santiago called. "Dex, stay with me!"

He tried to rise, to respond, to see, but it was just too much effort.

"Dex..."

Chapter Twelue

"Dex!" Vaughn Hollister had thrown himself flat on the cliff and was leaning over the edge to look at his son. "Dex, are you all right?"

Dex squeezed down tightly on his thigh as if he could strangle the pain into submission. He kept his head down, not to protect his face from the tumbling pebbles still shaking loose from his fall, but so his father would not see his tears. "I broke my leg, Dad," he shouted.

"Simple or compound?"

"Simple," he hollered, though he didn't see anything simple about his predicament.

"Can you climb?"

Was his old man crazy? "No, I can't climb!"

"Easy. You may have to. There are warblers about, and if they see us in their territory... I'm going to lower a rope. You know how to put it around you."

"I need a splint, Dad!"

"There's no time. Now man up. Here comes the rope—and keep quiet!"

That last was a hiss, but Dex didn't need the warning. He'd seen the shadow of the warbler flow over his legs.

He looked up, reaching with one hand. The heavy climbing cable lowered, snagged on the outcropping, then swung and lowered again as his dad fed it down. He stretched, because he knew he needed to, because his dad would expect nothing less than his best effort despite the pain, and grasped the lowered loop. He pulled it down and tucked it under his arms, and then jerked the line to signal he was ready.

His father pulled, offering support while letting him determine the speed of ascent. Dex climbed with his good leg and his arms, trying to keep any weight off the broken leg, but that didn't stop it from banging against the rocks. Each blow brought a new experience of agony. Colors flashed before his eyes; his jaw ached from clenching it so tightly. The rope dug at his armpits through the T-shirt. He blinked sweat and tears from his eyes but didn't dare let go of the cliff to wipe his face. The rope cut into him with steady pressure as his father silently urged him to keep climbing.

He chanced a glance up. Twenty-five feet at least before his father could grab him and haul him up. He couldn't make it. He had to make it. How could he make it?

His hand slipped, and the foot of his broken leg landed hard on a projecting rock. He cried out in pain.

His cry was answered by a shout—not his father's.

The warbler's.

It sounded so close. He twisted his face away from the cliff wall and yelped. It was mere feet from him, moving in an undulating hover as it backwinged to keep its position. It twisted its head, birdlike, to look from his face to his leg—now a full-fledged compound fracture—and back to his face.

He'd never been so close to a live warbler. He didn't know if it was the pain, the shock, or sheer reflex, but he saw every detail crystal-clear. A female, not long after weaning a brood, judging from her lean form. The mountain breeze ruffled each individual hair, making iridescent waves over the ocean of its wings. The tiny teeth were yellowed, yet glossy; its dinner-plate-sized eye not just brown, but with a greenish ring. The nostrils at the top of her beak flared as she examined his scent as well as his appearance. She had three long scars on her cheek; some prey hadn't gone down without a fight.

For a timeless moment, the two hung there, eyeing each other in curiosity and wonder.

"Dex!" His father called. "Brace yourself on the cliff so I can grab my gun!"

"No!" he shouted. "It's okay, Dad! I..."

He didn't know what he'd planned to say. He reached out with one hand toward the warbler.

"Dex, no!"

The warbler startled and with a powerful flap of its wings, ascended.

Dex grabbed its leg.

A dizzying ascent, so fast, he barely had time to gasp, then the warbler diving toward his father. He let go and fell onto the older man, who took the force of the fall and hugged him tightly.

Then his father was laughing and calling him an idiot with such pride in his voice that Dex couldn't help but smile as the grayness turned to black.

"Dex? Dex, stay with me..."

"Dex! Stay with me. You have to wake up."

Dex followed Santiago's voice out of the blackness and found himself in his control room, with a cargo bot supporting him. It must have dragged him from the airlock. Why hadn't it put him in a chair? Meanwhile, his last repair bot had abandoned its programmed task to remove his helmet and gloves and repair the tear in his suit. He blinked dully at the medical patch on his wrist— adrenaline and painkillers, he guessed. The bot hovered before him, holding the jury-rigged VR set.

The warbler... His broken leg must have triggered the memory.

The ship shook, dispelling the last of his confused lethargy. The ships were under attack; the bot was holding him in place so he wouldn't get tossed about. Santiago was fighting and needed his help.

He grabbed the gear and pulled it on. "How long?" he asked Santiago as he fitted the VR goggles into place.

"A little over three minutes. My capture beam has been disabled."

"Vac!" He glared at the small bot hovering in front of him. "Well, get on it!"

It sped away, and he activated the controls.

The world around him grew, changed color, and came alive with flashes of light and streaking phantoms of dark, and he was with Santiago, seeing through his sensors, feeling the impact of radiation and energy on his hull. The hiss and squeal of X-rays and other emissions pounded in his ears.

"Noise off," he commanded. He didn't have time to filter. Santiago and their captured ship had destroyed three of the drones, but the others were learning. They had moved out of the targeting area of Santiago's laser; he would only be able to aim by moving as well, straining the grapplers and the remaining capture beam. Nonetheless, the AI was using the laser to its best effect, laying a covering pattern that would keep the drones themselves away from where they could target the backup engineering section.

"Good work, my friend," Dex muttered. "But we're not going to win at this rate."

"I would be happy with a draw."

Dex made a disparaging noise, although he felt much the same. His gloved fingers moved, directing the sensor equipment Santiago had managed to attach to the captured ship's nose. "We won't get out of this thinking small."

"We wouldn't have gotten into this if we'd 'thought smaller.'" Santiago replied.

"Nag, nag." Damn, his leg throbbed! If this had been a true VR recording, he could have upped the settings to drown it out; instead, it remained a constant reminder of his folly.

But he wouldn't let it be a distraction. He scanned the area, called up a plot of their path. "Yes! Our prey isn't so helpless, yet. See the swarls?"

"I have seen them, but I've not been able to do much about them. Our current course will brush right by them, but without the capture beam..."

"Forget the beam. We're not pushing the drones into the swarls—we're going to ride the swarls out of here."

A pause. Again, the ship jerked and shuddered as Santiago jerked away from a laser shot Dex hadn't seen, then suffered the brunt of the explosion it caused on their prey. The bot held him mostly steady, but his leg wiggled, and for a moment, he fought his own battle against a red miasma of pain.

Still, he knew the silence came not from Santiago's concentration on the battle, but on his calculating their odds and seeking alternatives.

"I don't think it can maneuver that well," Santiago finally said.

"Then we have to push it. Pull in the grapplers and the other capture beam. Get in close as you can. Show me the swarls."

"I need those sensors to target the laser."

"Forget targeting. Just keep a covering fire and get ready to launch those torpedoes."

"Without the sensors..." But a clearer map of the swarls presented itself on Dex's headset. A perfect clockwork. He started to trace a route. If they could catch the current, ride it up and out...

"We're going to use them to clear our path. Be ready to push this beast into the swarl. Can you perfect the course?" His question ended in a gasp as the Santiago didn't so much jerk as bounce, causing his legs to rise then fall back against the floor.

"Hull breach, small airlock and adjoining storage," the computer reported. "Blocking off areas."

"Drone targeted—direct hit," Santiago chimed in. Despite everything, Dex imagined he heard a smug tone in the AI's voice. The ship rocked, a larger, flowing motion that made Dex suspect their prey had moved that time. He fought the temptation to turn the sensor focus away from the swarl to the battle. His skin crawled with phantom images as he imagined the drones swarming and piercing the ships with their directed energy. The wild flow of matter from the swarl grew closer.

"Perfect the course!"

"I can multitask. But with imprecise sensors and all our damage..."

"Do it!"

"Firing torpedo. Engaging thrusters. Brace yourself."

He grabbed the arms of the cargo bot as the *Santiago* applied all its power toward turning the captured ship on which they depended. He felt his ship's efforts in the vibrations of the deck; then, a sudden weight pressed him against flooring and robot as they were caught in the swarl.

"You did it!"

He opened his eyes and saw the familiar rush and sway of a swirling matter stream. Inside or outside the event horizon. A swarl was a swarl. His lips curled back against his teeth. "Pursuers?"

"Four." In one corner of his vision, a breakaway schematic showed the drones, small blips ravaging the larger pill-shaped indicator that represented the *Santiago* and the captured ship. Small lances of light flowed from them, twisting strangely in the varying gravities of the swarl, yet visuals and the shaking of the ship proclaimed hits nonetheless. In front of them, a single black line signified the event horizon and escape.

"Dex, do you see what I see?"

Dex focused on the section Santiago highlighted. The fire and debris of the torpedo expanded—then pulled in. The stream around it began to twist into a new swarl.

"Hard over!" Dex yelled, but Santiago was already pushing the ship up and away from the cosmic disturbance caused by the torpedo. The drones followed, but one didn't turn in time and was pulled apart by the quantum singularity, adding its mass to the wild, curving stream.

"Well, one mystery solved," Santiago commented dryly. The bizarre anomalies in Lincoln Eriadne, the fluxes and swarls, had been caused by the alien weaponry.

Dex scanned the twisting matter and radiation. They'd come to a curve soon, a twisting sine wave that would propel them up. If they could time it, however, they might also shake their pursuers—and maybe destroy a few. "Get that next torpedo ready. I want it out and starboard on my signal." His hands flew before him, one tracing the *Santiago's* projected path, the other breaking away to show his planned route for the weapon.

"Right into the pod of drones," he muttered, "and no way for them to avoid it without getting thrown back the way we came. Ready? At your best time, my friend."

"Ready. Approaching new current..."

Dex's breathing sounded loud to his ears. The ship had stilled. The drones were slowing—did they suspect? But they continued in their pursuit, just as he'd anticipated.

"Launching torpedo. Hard to port. They're firing on us!"

The shock of motion threw Dex to the floor. A gravitational surge ripped the goggles from his head and one VR glove from his hand. He could hear the computer saying something about another hull breach as Santiago called out three hits and damage, the shields failing.

"Dex—suit up!"

The repair bot flew to him, his suit gloves in its grasp. He yanked them on and reached for his helmet.

"Santiago! Talk to me! Shields?" He threw on the helmet and pressed the seals shut.

"Event horizon in nine...eight..."

Gravitational forces took hold of every cell in his body and pulled, and the last of Santiago's countdown was drowned out by his screams.

Everything around him, everything within him, tore, and he felt himself set afire then extinguished in the vacuum of space.

* * *

Dex woke up with his head in Scarlet's lap.

"Am I in heaven?" he murmured.

She stroked his hair. "You don't have a more original come-on than that?"

"I'm serious." But he couldn't put much energy into his protest. He wanted to look around—he tried to look around—but everything except Scarlet was bathed in a cool, white glow. He could sort-of see his body, but his eyes refused to focus beyond a general blur. Was it because he was still old, injured, and partly blind, or did his heavenly body need time to adjust to its surroundings? Scarlet, too, was little more than a hazy shadow backlit by brilliant light.

He closed his eyes, the better to concentrate on his tactile impressions, but answers continued to elude him. His body felt numb, anesthetized. He couldn't tell if he wore the young, strong body of his youth or the aching, traitorous one of his old age. His scalp tingled with every caress of Scarlet's fingers, but that offered no clues; even after 80-plus years, he'd kept all his hair.

"Feels nice," he murmured. "Heaven or hallucination, don't stop."

Scarlet chuckled, but there was a sadness to it. He forced his eyelids apart to look at her face. She remained blurred and shadowed, but he imagined he could sense the tension in her eyes and along her mouth.

He forced himself to a sitting position. "What's wrong?"

"I have to go."

"What? Where?"

She glanced behind her, to where the brilliance of light seemed to extend to infinity. "I stayed as long as you needed me."

"I do need you!"

She shook her head. "You've done the impossible, Dex. Again. As always. And I'm glad I was there to see it. But the path we walk together has ended. I have to go on alone."

He glanced at the light, and his blood ran cold with fear. "Are you saying...?"

He thought back to every fight, every insult, the way he'd thrown that useless apprentice out on his ear... How he'd ignored the signs of her disease until it was too late to do anything about it...

"Am I...?"

Her eyes widened, then she burst out in giggles. "No, Dex! Of course not. You're a good man at heart. You have more adventures ahead, things we never even dreamed of."

"Then let's go."

"Dex! I'm dead."

"Aren't I? I just crossed the event horizon of a black hole. Twice. I've had enough adventure. I'm tired. I want to go with you."

Suddenly, she stood before him. Her shadowy form crossed her arms and shifted weight to one hip in that way she did when exasperated but unwilling to compromise. "You can't get your way this time, Dex."

He blinked back the tears in his eyes. It's the light, he told himself. Practically a glare. If we just walk into it together, then I'd see her properly.

She took a step toward him, and he saw her. Perfectly, the way he'd always meant to see her. The way his heart always knew her to be.

And when she spoke, he marveled at the beauty of her voice, even as his heart broke at her words.

"I love you, Dex Hollister. Goodbye."

Epilogue

Hospital ward, Keldar Station
Unification Era 2.98.87

Georj Brenna stared wide-eyed at the figure swathed in regenerative healing cloths. "Amazement-empathic! A human from six hundred years ago, verification-query-emphatic."

The Elomijan doctor ruffled his short fur in the equivalent of a shrug. "Verification conditional. He awoke long enough to give a date, from the pre-unification era. He was retrieved among wreckage even older—of the Beforetime, when the People split and those desiring to war designed machines to battle in the Footprints of Hudon." He clawed his hand in a sign of warding.

Brenna nodded. His university paid dearly for the relic, both in credits and in lives lost when the ship powered itself up and fought like the demon thing of the tales the People told their children. But the People had grown in wisdom and technology since those fairytale days; the ship, already damaged, was not able to resist long. Now it rested in state in the Galand University museum, studied by engineers and historians who boasted of their luck as if Elomij had personally gifted them with the secrets of the Beforetime.

They could have the ship. Any secrets it held were as cold and barren as the metal of its hull. There, lying in the hospital bed just on the other side of the glass, was the true key to the secrets of the past. And Brenna was one of the few people in the parsec who would be able to communicate with him.

A nurse stood over the sleeping ancient, spreading a healing salve over the fabric. It contained a cocktail of genetic resequencing nanites and chemicals that would restore and modify the man's horribly damaged body. She finished her ministrations, checked the monitors, and with a nod toward the two-way glass, left the room.

"You said his brain will be healed as well? Will he know our language?"

A snicker from the doctor confirmed his suspicion. "We are challenged enough to heal him, much less educate him."

Yet... "He gave you a date? How?"

Again, the doctor's fur rippled.

However, the nurse spoke from the doorway. "He spoke our language as if born to it. He is the goddess-chosen. The Huntradex." She bowed as she spoke the name.

Brenna turned from her and leaned closer to the glass. "Amazement-emphatic."

The Adventure Continues in Dex's Way

Find out what happens to Dex and Santiago in this strange future world. Get Dex's Way on Amazon and read on.

Sign up for Karina's newsletter at https://fabianspace.substack.com/subscribe to discover all her upcoming books.

So many thanks!

Way too many years ago, I was between novels and feeling bored, so I asked my husband to challenge me. He suggested I write a science fiction book based on *The Old Man and the Sea* by Earnest Hemingway. I spent a couple of weeks studying Hemingway's novella, then mapped out my own adventure. *The Old Man and the Void* is the result. You'll see similarities in the plot and structure, but I did add my own flare.

Of course, adding "flare" also meant adding some complexities to the Hemingway's elegant plot. Matthew Bowman and Michelle Buckman are both highly skilled editors who looked over this book out of friendship and love of our craft and gave suggestions for improving flow. I am very grateful for their time and advice. If you are an author looking for a strong editor, contact me and I'll get you their info.

This book's manuscript is so old, it's been through two crit groups. Many thanks to my (now defunct) Thariss Tuus group, and to my current CWG SFF crit pals. You gave me sound, specific advice. Overall, these people took this book from really good (IM-HO) to really great. Also, thanks to beta readers Annette Tenny, John Earle, and Michael Bertrand. Thanks, guys!

Dawn Grimes took my generic idea for the cover and made it awesome and energetic. She does the Space Traipse covers, too. You're awesome, Dawn!

About the Author

Karina was born in Colorado but has lived in three countries and 11 states. She graduated from Colorado State University with a degree in mathematics and a commission in the USAF, which let her see the world. She married fellow officer, Rob Fabian. She left the Air Force when her first child was born to enjoy the military life as a spouse while pursuing writing.

After Rob retired as a colonel, they moved to Florida, where he became COO of Vaya Space. Thus, Karina writes science fiction while he works to make science fact. It's a perfect relationship.

She has published dozens of books, from serious science fiction to humorous fantasy and comedic horror. She also writes nonfiction and software reviews. You can find a list of her books at https://karinafabian.com.

There's More Fun in FabianSpace

Thank you for buying this book. If you enjoyed it, click to see the others in this series or discover one of the other worlds of FabianSpace.

Science Fiction
Space Traipse: Hold My Beer: Redneck ingenuity and common sense in a Star Trek-ish universe. Enjoy the adventures of the HMB Impulsive.
The Rescue Sisters: Intrepid women doing dangerous missions in space for the love of God and humankind.
The Old Man and the Void: Dex is a relic hunter on the edge of the black hole, desperate for the catch of a lifetime.
Jovian Heat: As the next Great Storm of Jupiter rises, Cass must find the father of a baby in peril—but the father died before the child was conceived.

Fantasy
DragonEye: Vern's a snarky dragon on the wrong side of the Interdimensional Gap, solving crimes, battling evil, and saving the universes on an all-too-regular basis.
Madness of Kanaan: Deryl isn't crazy; he's psychic, and aliens of two worlds thinks he can save them. Maybe he can—but can he regain his sanity in the process?

Horror
Neeta Lyffe, Zombie Exterminator: Neeta's an average exterminator, taking out bugs, rodents, and the undead. Can she keep her friends alive, pay her bills, and find romance?
Frightliner and Other Tales of the Supernatural (with Colleen Drippé): Truck-driving vampires, zombie weddings and more.